Lemon Chiffon

LITTLE CAKES, BOOK TWO

PEPPER NORTH

PAIGE MICHAELS

Copyright © 2022 by Pepper North & Paige Michaels

All characters and events in this book are fictitious. And resemblance to actual persons living or dead is strictly coincidental. The characters are all over the age of 18 and as adults choose to live their lives in an age play environment. All rights reserved.

No part of this book may be reproduced in any form or by any electronic or mechanical means, including information storage and retrieval systems, without written permission from the author, except for the use of brief quotations in a book review.

This is a series of books that can be read in any order. You may, however, choose to read them sequentially to enjoy the characters best. Subsequent books will feature characters that appear in previous novels as well as new faces.

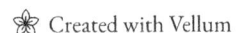

❦ Created with Vellum

About the Book

Welcome to Little Cakes, the bakery that plays Daddy matchmaker! Little Cakes is a sweet and satisfying series, but dare to taste only if you like delicious Daddies, luscious Littles, and guaranteed happily-ever-afters.

Daisy Galante adores hanging out with the Littles at Blaze until she meets creepy member Leo. While escaping the pretend Daddy's unwarranted punishment, she is rescued by her friend and dungeon master, Tarson.

Stern, ex-military cupcake baker, Tarson Kirkwood, is enchanted by the delicate floral shop owner. His attempts to remain friends only are squashed that night at the club. When his newly claimed Little is in danger, he'll reveal that his nickname Teddy Bear disguises a fiercely protective grizzly side.

Chapter One

"I love how it smells in here!" Erica announced as she walked into the floral shop.

"Hi, Erica! I'm glad you're here. I just got a big order for a wedding. Their first choice of florist has an out-of-business sign on their door," Daisy shared, rolling her eyes. "I know everyone is looking for a bargain, but really! Choose someone reliable."

"Was that The Perfect Petal? I thought I had breaking news to share."

"Yep! They went belly up. I hate to see people lose their shop, even if they are my competition. Start making boutonnieres. I made one as a model. It's on the bench there," Daisy waved a hand toward the floral design table.

"How many do we need?"

"Twenty-eight. And that's just the boutonnieres. I haven't even started on the bouquets." Daisy tried to prevent her eyes from rolling again. She ended up looking cross-eyed, provoking a laugh from her assistant.

"There are that many men in the ceremony?"

"Yes. It's a massive wedding." Daisy read from her list on the wall in front of her. "There are eleven groomsmen, the groom, four fathers—the bride and groom both have a father and a stepfather—three grandfathers, four ushers, a flower boy, a ring bearer, and one male reader. We'll make two extras because someone is bound to destroy theirs before the wedding."

"Why do I want to sing 'And a partridge in a pear tree' at the end of that?" Erica joked.

"Because you have a quirky sense of humor that compliments your floral skills," Daisy complimented as she pressed roses into the massive wedding bouquet. The order would make her monthly numbers look a lot better, but she'd be living in the store until everything was complete.

"When's the wedding?" Erica asked, studying the simple design Daisy had crafted.

"Tomorrow."

"Holy crap! Let's get working." Erica immediately walked into the floral storage area for supplies.

Daisy looked after her assistant and smiled. She'd worked with her mother since Daisy had been old enough not to bruise the flowers as she sniffed them. When her parents decided to move to Florida, the store had been lonely. Erica's brass personality livened it up—a lot.

"Don't work all night, Daisy. Go home," Erica directed as she hung up her apron. "I'm sorry I can't stay later. I'll come back early in the morning to finish up the order."

Daisy waved her off. "Don't worry. I'm just glad we close at five on Sundays. At least I won't have customers coming in after you leave. You can't miss your dad's birthday party! I'll just get a couple more bouquets done and then I'm out of here," Daisy promised. Sometimes, Erica was more of a mom than her mother had been.

Erica pulled out her phone and took a picture of Daisy. "If you're in the same clothes tomorrow when I get here…"

"You!" Daisy made shooing motions to hurry along her assistant.

When the door closed behind Erica, she turned back to the bouquet. She had no intention of leaving until the last of the bouquets were done. It might take her half the night, but she knew she wouldn't be able to sleep if this job wasn't finished.

A while later, she glanced at the clock. Six o'clock. She was making good time. There were still a lot of bouquets to arrange, but she was determined.

"How many more of these do I still need?" Daisy asked herself, propping a hip against the table for support. Each rose felt like it weighed five pounds.

She jumped as the back door abruptly opened and smacked the wall. Daisy tried to control her facial expression to not show panic as four men invaded her store.

"We're closed, gentlemen."

"Really? I think you'll open to let us smell the roses," one man said with an evil laugh. The others echoed him.

"We're here to provide protection for you. You know—keep the bad guys away."

"Thank you, but I'm sure I'm fine here without your help," she answered, moving a hand toward the pruning shears she used to cut the stems.

"No need to arm yourself, lady," the ringleader commented as he snatched the would-be weapon. "You and I are going to stand here real safe as the guys find our fee."

When Daisy opened her mouth to protest, the man waved the shears. "I bet this would take off a finger. Would that make it tough to arrange flowers?"

Cringing at the thought, Daisy dropped her hands down to the workbench and watched helplessly as the men ransacked her store looking for money. "I already went to the bank. I don't have anything here."

He just glared at her with a deadly stare. One by one, the

men returned to stand at his flanks. Each shook their heads as they joined the group.

"Nothing but flowers," one remarked.

"I think we'll each take one of these," the spokesman announced, reaching a hand for a completed bridesmaid bouquet.

Daisy's heart sank as she watched the men each pick up a bouquet and bury their nose in it, deliberately crushing the delicate blossoms. One proceeded to create his own bridal path as he yanked petals from his arrangement to scatter over the ground. The others destroyed theirs in various ways to leave the floor covered in crushed floral carcasses.

"I hope the bride lives happily ever after," the leader laughed as the crew tromped through the back door.

Freed from her frozen position, Daisy flew to the back door to click the bolt into position. Fumbling for her phone, she dialed 911 as she raced to the cooler for more flowers. There was no time to cry. She still had so many bouquets to make and now her job was going to take even longer.

"911, what's your emergency?"

"Four men just walked in the back door of my floral shop and destroyed bouquets when they couldn't find any money," Daisy reported, blinking furiously to stop herself from crying as she grabbed a form to start a replacement bouquet.

"Do you have someone who can come stay with you? I'm sending officers to take a report, but they won't be there for a while," the operator asked. She must have heard the emotion in Daisy's voice.

An immediate image of a muscular man popped into her mind. Daisy always felt safe with him around. "I'll call a friend," she promised the operator.

After thanking the emergency responder, Daisy searched her phone to find a number she'd saved. It rang twice, and she hung up. *I don't want to bother him. He's probably busy.*

Daisy set the phone on her workbench with a shake of her

head. Tarson Kirkwood—everyone called him Bear—took care of everyone at Blaze. He wasn't her personal security force.

When her phone buzzed loudly on the table, Daisy snapped the stem of a carnation in half as she jumped. Snatching the phone up, she automatically answered, "Blooms by Daisy."

"What's up, Daisy? Are you okay?" Bear's deep voice sounded concerned.

"I'm sorry, Bear. I shouldn't have called. My shop was just vandalized by a group of men." Daisy tried to keep her voice steady, but a quiver betrayed her.

"Did you call the police?" he demanded.

She could hear something rustling through the connection. "I did. The police are coming to file a report. The dispatcher suggested I call someone to stay with me. For some reason, my fingers chose you to call. Then I realized how stupid it was to disturb you, so I hung up. I'm sorry."

"I'm on my way. I'll call you when I'm at the back door."

"No, Bear. Really. I'm okay," she reassured him as she dropped her forehead down to rest on the cool counter. Daisy tried to pull herself together.

"I'll make sure of that myself. Five minutes, Little girl. I'll be right there."

Daisy stared at the cellphone. He'd hung up. Glancing at the clock to estimate what time he would be there, she worked quickly to create another bouquet. With each flower and stem of greenery she added, Daisy forced the panic to stay at bay. After four minutes, her phone rang again.

"Bear?"

"I'm here, Daisy. Come let me in."

Daisy flew across the work area, threw the door open, and stared at the muscular man dressed in grey sweatpants and a blue T-shirt. Unable to stop herself, she rushed forward to press herself against him. His arms wrapped around her to hold her close. Daisy closed her eyes and laid her head on his broad chest.

"Thank you for coming. I was so scared."

His hands glided over her back to reassure her. "I'm glad you called. Let's go inside and you can tell me what's going on."

When she didn't move, Bear lifted her easily in a giant hug and walked forward, allowing the door to slam behind him. He set Daisy's feet back on the ground and turned to flip the lock back into place. Scanning the debris cluttering the floor, he nudged a destroyed bouquet with his toe.

"That has to be bad luck for the wedding," he suggested with an arched eyebrow.

Daisy backed away from him self-consciously. "I got this big order. Their scheduled florist went out of business right before the wedding. I was working on the bridesmaids' bouquets when four men came in the door. This is what they did when I didn't have any money for them to steal."

"What can I do to help?"

"Could you just stay with me until the police get here? I'm here all the time alone, but I'm..."

"Not alone now," he finished. "Work. I'll take some pictures. After the police leave, I'll clean up this mess."

"You don't have to do that," she protested.

"Work. Make something beautiful like you always do."

Nodding, Daisy dashed back to her work area. Bear repeatedly drew her attention as he strode through the mess on the floor to check the door and look outside. When the police knocked and announced themselves, he opened it and showed the officers inside.

"I'm Tarson Kirkwood, a friend of Daisy Galante. She called me after she talked to the 911 operator."

"I'm Daisy," she said, walking forward to meet the officers.

After they introduced themselves, one asked, "I don't suppose you have security cameras?"

Daisy clapped her hands together. She hadn't thought about the cameras. "Flowers rarely put up a fight, but yes. I do. Maybe that will help catch them. The owner of the strip center might have some video too."

"Who's the owner?"

With Garrett Erickson's information recorded, the other policeman asked, "Can you tell us what happened?"

Running through the story, Daisy tried to stay unemotional, but the invasion and destruction had taken a toll. When a familiar warmth approached her from behind, she backed up to lean against Teddy's—*um, Bear's*—hard body. She mentally corrected herself. Daisy needed to remember not to call him by the nickname some Littles used at Blaze, the BDSM club they belonged to. Her hand reached back for his and she unwound the tiniest fraction more when Bear linked his fingers with hers.

"I'll file a report, Ms. Galante. Be sure to contact your insurance to make a claim for damages. There have been other incidents with this group. They seem to take advantage of unlocked doors, so stay vigilant about securing rear entrances—especially in off hours when no one's around," one police officer suggested.

"Thank you, sir. Believe me, I'm going to lock the door next time."

When they left, Bear moved silently around the workroom to remove the trashed remains of the wedding bouquets. Unable to give in to the fright, Daisy went back to work, determined to recreate the bouquets she'd lost and finish the orders. "You don't have to stay with me, Bear. I'll be fine."

Bear frowned at her. "I'm not leaving you here alone, Little girl."

"It will probably take me most of the night to complete this order. I don't want to put you out."

He narrowed his gaze at her. "Daisy, you do realize I'm a Daddy, right?"

She swallowed, nodding.

"What kind of Daddy would I be if I left a Little girl alone in her shop all night after a break-in?"

"Okay," she whispered. She had a lot of work to do, and her

adrenaline was pumping hard. She was grateful that Teddy stayed to help clean up and keep her company.

Daisy jumped in her spot and turned around to stare at the back door many hours later when it opened.

Daisy blew out a breath of relief when she realized it was Erica. Was it morning already?

"I was joking about you still being here in the same clothes, Daisy." Erica laughed. "Did you fall asleep?"

When Bear moved into view, Erica exclaimed, "Wow! Maybe sleep wasn't what kept you from making bouquets."

"Erica, this is Tarson. He came to stay with me after some men broke into the shop last night."

Erica gasped, her eyes wide with concern. "You were still working?"

"I was working on the bridesmaids' arrangements. When the men didn't find money to steal, they destroyed several bouquets."

"On it. Let's get these finished." Erica didn't ask any more questions. She immediately got started.

Daisy knew Erica would inundate her with questions when the order was finished, but she'd shelved everything for now to concentrate on getting the arrangements done. Smiling gratefully at her irreplaceable assistant, Daisy tugged Bear to the back door.

"Thank you for coming to stay with me. I was pretty petrified," Daisy confessed. "You were the best friend."

"Call me if you need me again," Bear sternly directed.

Daisy picked up that Bear wasn't manifesting the dungeon master role he assumed at Blaze. That's who he was—fierce and protective. She nodded, "I will."

"Oh, and Little girl, I'm not interested in being a friend."

She stared at him, unable to form a coherent answer to that statement. When he lowered his head to kiss her softly, there was no mistaking his meaning. Daisy clung to his broad shoulders, only releasing him when Bear stepped away.

"Go make beautiful flowers, happy Little girl," he said as he disappeared through the door.

When it clicked behind him, Erica whistled low. "I'm going to have to make it cooler in here. That was hot."

Chapter Two

Daisy hesitated outside Blaze. She hadn't been to the club since the store invasion. Her thoughts had examined that kiss from all angles and she'd decided either Bear's kiss meant he was interested in her or he'd just been reassuring a Little. Scared to find out which one it was, she'd avoided asking him every time he called.

Finally, Daisy decided she had to know. She'd driven like a wild woman to Blaze so she didn't have time to talk herself out of going. Forcing herself out of the car, she straightened her braids over her shoulders and walked to the door. A new face answered the door.

"Password, please."

"Um... Flames?" Daisy suggested hesitantly. Bear was always there to recognize her and let her inside. She hadn't used the password for a long time.

"That seems to be everyone's answer today. Looks like Tarson let the passcode slide from everyone's mind," the younger man observed.

"Bear's the best. He knows everyone," Daisy leapt to the dungeon master's defense. She knew some of the other Doms and Daddies called Bear by his real name, Tarson, but most people referred to him as Bear. Secretly, most of the Littles called him Teddy.

"Whoa, Little girl. I'm not criticizing. Tarson obviously recognized everyone. He wasn't able to man the door tonight. He's decorating cupcakes, of all things, and will be here later. I'm Hector. What's your name?"

"I'm Daisy. Sorry. I forgot Bear was working for Ellie tonight. Thanks for taking his place." Even though Bear was often the dungeon monitor at Blaze, he liked to work at the door early in the evening beforehand to see who all came in.

"I'm glad to be here. Come in. There're a few Littles playing a game in the daycare. It looks like fun. Evan is filling in as dungeon monitor until Bear arrives. I'll be at the door if you need anything."

"Thanks." Daisy headed for the section devoted to the Littles. They were playing Simon Says with a guy at the club who'd decided he was a Daddy. Daisy had some reservations about him. Maybe she was judging him too quickly. It was possible she was still jumpy after her encounter with the four thugs. She suddenly felt suspicious of everyone.

"Hey, Daisy. I'd hoped to see you tonight. Come join us," the man greeted her. "Remember me? I'm Daddy Leo."

"Hi, Daddy Leo," Daisy greeted him obediently as she joined the line of Littles standing in front of him.

"Simon says, hands on your butt!" Leo called.

Everyone quickly shifted their arms to press their palms against their buttocks. Daisy didn't like that Leo's gaze focused on all the Littles' breasts. *Had he done that on purpose? Am I imagining it?*

"Simon says, jump up and down."

Daisy thanked her athletic bra that compressed and held her in place. Some Littles giggled as they bounced all over. Others looked as uncomfortable as she felt.

"Stop!"

Immediately, Daisy froze in place. She knew she'd knocked

herself out of the game because he hadn't started with Simon Says.

"Oh, no, Daisy. I didn't say Simon Says. You were supposed to keep jumping," Leo corrected her. "You must not have known the rules, right?" He winked at her conspiratorially. "You can have one free mistake."

The other Littles protested, and Daisy quickly agreed with them. "No, that's okay. I like to play by the rules. I think I'll go color." She wandered over to the table and took a seat with her back to the group.

As Daddy Leo eliminated other Littles, the coloring table became more popular. Soon, the conversation about their designs drowned out the instructions coming from behind Daisy. She relaxed, enjoying the company of her friends.

"Daisy, I came to see you tonight." Daddy Leo's voice grated on her ears. It wasn't the Daddy voice she wanted to hear.

"That's nice. I love spending time with this group." Daisy tried to deflect his statement to include everyone.

"Little girl, you're not listening to me. Come with me right now. We are going to talk about this privately."

As a hush fell over the assembled Littles, Leo grabbed her forearm and stood, yanking Daisy to her feet. He pulled her with him as he left the daycare area.

"Daisy, do you want me to get help?" a concerned Little asked as the others looked on with wide stunned eyes. No one treated Littles like that at Blaze.

"I'll just talk to him. It will be okay." Daisy didn't want to get anyone in trouble. Maybe some Littles liked to have rough Daddies. She'd just explain to Leo.

Entering a secluded alcove, Leo sat and pulled her between his thighs. "You have been very bad, Little girl. I'll have to spank your bottom to correct your behavior."

Daisy fought off his hands as he tried to unfasten her jeans. "No, I don't want you to be my Daddy," she hissed, trying to stay quiet. He'd get thrown out of the club forever if she made a fuss.

A deep voice caught her attention. Bear had arrived. He'd make his usual rounds through the club before taking over for Evan. Daisy thought about calling his name but didn't want to get Leo in trouble. *This has to be just a misunderstanding, right?*

"Ouch!" Her distraction had prevented her from dodging as Leo spanked her bottom through her jeans. Stinging pain filled her mind.

"Littles need to follow their Daddies' instructions, Daisy. Stop this right now. I've seen how you've watched me."

"I haven't been," she assured him. "You must have misunderstood. Just let me go and I won't say anything."

"Hey, Leo. Where'd you go? The Littles are all over me. They're concerned about Daisy," Evan's voice called from the main corridor. From the sound of his voice, she could tell he was searching each area for her.

"Stay here. I'll send him on his way."

Daisy watched him walk to the entrance of the alcove and step slightly into the hallway. Without hesitating, she dashed behind him and escaped to the bar. Hiding behind the wooden counter, she whispered to Riley, "Don't react. Get Bear."

In just a few minutes, the immense man walked in as he checked over the club. Daisy was relieved when Riley suddenly invented a reason to get him to the bar.

Chapter Three

"Hey, Dungeon Master. I've got a new whiskey for you to sample," Riley called across the social gathering area of Blaze as Tarson walked in to look around.

"I don't drink while I'm on duty," he answered curtly. Everyone knew that was the rule.

"At least come sniff this. You'll want to come back after your shift is over." She coaxed him to approach.

"Sniff it?" Tarson shook his head as he walked her way. Had Riley been drinking too much? That wasn't like her at all. As he approached, she waved him around the bar.

"Careful. Glance down, but try not to look obvious," Riley whispered to him from the corner of her mouth as she held the bottle toward his nose.

"Check this out," she announced louder for the crowd gathered around the bar.

Instantly, Tarson's warning radar sounded. Something wasn't right here. As he dipped his head to sniff, Tarson saw a huddled figure pressed as small as possible against the wooden barrier.

"Teddy?" A small sound whispered from the back of the bar. "Can you get me out of here? I'm scared."

Daisy! The nickname the Littles didn't think he knew about clued him in on how frightened she had to be. He dropped a hand down to stroke over her silky blonde hair to reassure her. Tarson didn't stop to question why she was hiding. The Little had a good reason.

"That smells amazing, Riley. I'll look forward to sampling it soon."

Tarson walked to the supply cabinet and grabbed a folded black tablecloth. Nonchalantly walking back to the bar, he searched for a way to create a distraction. A flash of movement captured his attention as Blaze's resident shibari expert appeared. Milo's rope demonstrations were extremely popular.

"Hey, Knot Master! When's the next performance? Weren't you looking for volunteers?" Tarson sacrificed the experienced member to the eager crowd. He'd apologize later.

As everyone swarmed to speak to Milo Dante, Tarson wrapped the tablecloth around Daisy and carried her into the office unseen. Sitting down in the large chair, he freed the small figure from the material. The sight of her tear-stained face thrust a stake through his heart. Instantly, he was ready to pounce on whoever had hurt her.

"Teddy!" Daisy threw herself against his chest and wrapped her arms around his neck, holding on tightly. "I knew you'd help me!"

"Baby girl. Who do I need to kill?" Tarson growled, his protective instincts on the verge of a rampage.

"Just hold me. I'll be okay. He just spooked me. I should have handled it better," she rushed to reassure him.

"No one should scare a Little. Who was it?"

"I don't want to tell you his name. I'm sure he was just playing too hard."

"Name, Baby girl."

She blinked her pretty blue eyes at him. "He called himself Daddy Leo. I don't know him well."

"I know him."

Tarson shifted to pull his walkie-talkie from his belt. Phones were not allowed inside the club to avoid pictures being shared of play. "Evan, find Leo Miller and escort him from the club. He's no longer a member of Blaze."

"What reason do I tell him?" Evan's voice sounded tinny over the device.

"He'll know. Oh, and Hector is still monitoring the entrance. Fill him in about Leo, please."

"Will do."

With that, Tarson turned off the sound and tossed the walkie on the desk. He ran his hands lightly over her body, checking for anything sore. "Did he hurt you?"

"No. He wanted to spank me, but I didn't like it. He only managed one rough swat. I don't even know why he thought I needed a spanking," Daisy protested.

"Good job, Baby girl. Next time, you yell," he instructed.

"I didn't want to ruin everyone else's fun."

A knock came at the door and it opened before Tarson could respond. Evan leaned inside as Daisy hid her face against Tarson's chest. "She okay, boss? The asshole's gone. Davis is spending time with the Littles to calm them down. He walked in at just the right time."

"Good. Davis will make sure everyone is okay. He'll read everyone a story." Tarson knew the handsome silver fox with the kind voice and impeccable manners would reassure everyone.

"I've got the floor for the night," Evan assured him. Tarson understood the message from the floor monitor that he should take his time with Daisy.

"Thank you, Evan."

"Little girl," Evan called for Daisy's attention.

When she turned her head to meet his gaze, Evan said softly, "None of this is your fault. According to all the Littles, you didn't provoke his treatment in any way."

He started to close the door behind him but turned to look

back inside at her. "Yell next time. I feel like I let you down. I'll be more alert in the future."

The door clicked into place before she could answer. Daisy looked at Tarson with a bewildered expression. "It wasn't his fault that Leo wasn't right to be my Daddy. I couldn't do what he wanted me to do."

"I'm glad you listened to what your heart and head told you," Tarson said as he gently rocked her in the office chair. His lips brushed her forehead.

"Teddy?" she asked hesitantly.

"Yes, Baby girl?"

"I really only wanted to see you tonight. That's why I came," she blurted in a rush of words.

"You could have told me that during one of the times I called to check on you," Tarson reminded her with the mention of their phone conversations after the invasion. He'd needed to make sure she was okay. Each time, she'd seemed distant and too busy to talk.

"I didn't want you to feel obligated."

"There's a difference between a kind friend caring that you're happy and safe and someone who truly wants to be involved in your life."

"Are you telling me you want to be more than a friend?"

"Yes, Baby girl. I told you that. I want to be much more. Can you see me as part of your life?"

"Yes," she whispered.

"That makes me very happy, Little girl."

Tarson squeezed her close as he continued to rock her on his lap. She felt perfect in his arms. Mentally, he cursed Daddy Leo for touching what was his, while thanking him for being the catalyst to help Daisy be honest about her feelings.

"Do you feel better now?" he asked after a few minutes. He wished he could cuddle with her and take things to the next level. He'd been looking forward to spending more time with her for the past two days.

The timing was not right though. Not tonight. Not when she'd just been through a traumatic experience and he'd spent hours making cupcakes for tomorrow's opening day at Little Cakes. They both needed to go home and get some sleep—their own homes, unfortunately.

Soon he would want to bring her home with him and introduce her to the special nursery attached to the master bedroom. It still needed some finishing touches, but in between baking, he'd been filling that room with every special detail a Baby girl like Daisy would enjoy.

He'd had his eye on her for a while, but his feelings had flooded in and solidified the moment he stepped into her shop the other night. She'd been so flustered and shaken from having her space invaded.

His chest had tightened as soon as he heard her voice on the phone, so small and scared. And then when he'd set his eyes on her, he'd instantly known his feelings were not platonic. Not even close.

Daisy was his Baby girl.

He would pick up the pace getting the nursery ready because Friday night he fully intended to have her in his home. He would never pressure her to be intimate with him. They could take that side of things at whatever pace felt comfortable for her, but he wanted her under his roof in the nursery as soon as possible.

He tipped her head back and kissed her lips gently. That was as far as he would allow himself to take things tonight. "You should get home, Baby girl. You've had a rough night. Can I drive you?"

She stared into his eyes and shook her head slowly. "I have my own car," she whispered.

"Will you let me follow you then? I want to be sure you arrive there safely."

She blinked and then lowered her gaze. "Okay." Her voice was almost too soft to hear.

He cupped her face, rubbing her cheek with his thumb. "You seem disappointed. Were you hoping to stay and play with the other Littles a while longer?"

Another very slow head shake. "No."

"Look at me, Baby girl."

She lifted her gaze.

"Tell me what's upsetting you."

"I wanted to spend more time with you."

He smiled. "I'm so glad to hear that. And you will. But not tonight after you've been through a scare. Besides, I've been baking all day. I'm sure I smell like frosting." He tickled under her chin, hoping to get a smile out of her.

She giggled as she scrunched her neck. "You don't smell like frosting, Teddy."

He gave her a fake frown. "I'll never understand why you Littles started calling me Teddy. I'm more of a ferocious grizzly bear." He couldn't keep from grinning.

She covered her mouth as if she could stifle her giggles. "I'm afraid that's not true. Sorry, *Teddy*."

He pulled her closer and kissed the top of her head. There was no way to quell the nickname. He was stuck with it. Plus, if his Little girl wanted to think of him as a Teddy bear, then so be it. He intended to be a soft place for her to fall for the rest of their lives if she would have him.

Nope. He didn't mind being called Teddy, but he sure hoped one day soon she would start calling him Daddy instead.

Reluctantly, Tarson lifted her off his lap and set her on her feet. "Let's get you home, Baby girl."

She stuck out her lower lip in a pout. If circumstances were different, he would take her over his knee and spank her bottom. But not tonight. She'd already received a swat tonight from a fake Daddy. No way would Tarson add to the jarring experience.

Soon. He would make sure he managed to get his palm on her little bottom in the not-too-distant future.

He tipped her chin back with a finger and met her gaze with a stern look. "You get a free pass tonight, but you might want to keep that bottom lip tucked in next time, Little girl. As your Daddy, I won't hesitate to take you over my knee." He lifted a brow.

Her eyes widened. "Sorry, Teddy."

He rolled his eyes at the silly nickname, barely refraining from insisting on her calling him Daddy this time. *Soon*, he reminded himself. "Come on, Baby girl." He took her hand and led her from the office.

It was a test of his willpower to tuck her into her own car, buckle her seatbelt, and shut her door. He gripped the steering wheel of his SUV the entire time as he followed her home.

When they arrived at her condo, he took her keys from her, unlocked her door, and stepped inside without asking for permission. The Daddy in him insisted he make sure her place was safe before he left her.

After a quick look around, he turned to find her smiling just inside the front door. "Did you find any monsters, Teddy?"

The little imp was teasing him, and it was cute. He loved that she was playful and could make jokes after being terrorized just a short time ago. It spoke of her strong character.

Tarson strode back to where she stood, cupped her face, and gave her a light kiss. If he let himself get carried away, he'd never get out of here.

As he released her lips, he forced another stern look. "Better get used to me, Baby girl. I'll never risk you possibly being in a dangerous situation. After your confrontation with those thugs on Sunday night and your mistreatment by Leo tonight, I'm not likely to let you out of my sight more than necessary."

She swallowed. "You really mean it, Teddy?"

He nodded. It was obviously going to take some time to convince her she was his. "I really mean it, Baby girl. Now, lock this door behind me. I'll come by your shop tomorrow during the day when I visit Little Cakes' grand opening. I'm sure I'll have to work late tomorrow night making more cupcakes, but Friday night, I'm off. Save Friday night for me."

She smiled and then threw her arms around his waist and hugged him tight. "I hope this isn't a dream," she whispered.

He rubbed her back. "It's not a dream, Baby girl. I promise."

Chapter Four

Daisy was on top of the world when she arrived at her shop the next morning. She had slept well, considering how much was on her mind. Today, she was her usual sunny self—at least she liked to think of herself as a sunny person.

Even though she'd had an unpleasant experience at Blaze last night, her time spent with Teddy had erased enough of the bad encounter to calm her racing heart so she was able to snuggle under the covers and fall into a deep sleep.

After parking behind Blooms by Daisy and locking her car, she nearly skipped up to the back door. The moment she got close, her face fell and she abruptly stopped.

Her heart rate picked up in a hurry as she stared at the dead flowers lying at her back door. Not any random flowers, but the same ones Tarson had thrown into the dumpster Sunday night after those thugs had ruined several bouquets.

She inched slowly closer, glancing around in every direction, worried someone might be watching her. There was no mistaking the wilted buds, and as soon as she was directly over them, she realized the pile was actually one entire bouquet. The only thing missing was the ribbon she'd tied around the bunch of flowers.

Scared, Daisy quickly unlocked the back door, opened it, and slipped inside. Her fingers shook as she disarmed the alarm and then reset it. Normally she would leave the alarm off after arriving, but she needed to set it at least until Erica arrived today.

Squeezing her eyes shut, she tried to think what to do. She could call the police, but what good would it do to let them know there were some dead flowers at her back door? It sounded ridiculous. Maybe an animal dragged them out of the dumpster.

You don't believe that for a minute.

She should call Bear, but it was opening day for Little Cakes. The last thing she wanted to do was cause anyone undue stress on the big day.

Taking a deep breath, she decided to be brave. Go back outside, sweep the mess into a bag, and leave it to deal with later. She hurried to take care of it before Erica arrived so her employee wouldn't have to face the mess.

Nevertheless, Daisy was worried all morning. Not so much because she thought someone would bother her store in broad daylight, but because she knew when Bear found out, he wouldn't be happy.

Many times, she considered calling the police, but when she looked outside and saw the growing line waiting for Little Cakes to open, she knew it would ruin everything if the cops pulled up.

She waited until the afternoon when Erica was working the register, there was a lull in customers, and their afternoon help had arrived, to take a break. JT was amazing. He was a high school senior with an incredible eye for all things artistic who helped out two or three afternoons a week, often as her delivery driver.

Daisy wanted to visit Little Cakes and take some flowers as an opening-day gift. Or maybe that was just an excuse. She was secretly hoping to see Bear.

"I'll be back in fifteen minutes," she told Erica as she gathered the bouquet.

"Don't rush. Take a lunch break. You haven't left the shop all day. I'll be fine."

Daisy smiled. "We'll see what happens."

Hurrying past the few shops between Blooms by Daisy and Little Cakes, she couldn't wait to see how things were going. She knew Ellie—the owner—was both nervous and excited.

As she walked into the delicious aroma that filled the cupcake bakery, Daisy marveled at the bustling crowd. Chattering people filled almost every table. Their cheerful voices reflected their enjoyment of the delicious treats coming from the kitchen.

"Hi, Daisy!" Ellie exclaimed as Daisy stepped inside.

Daisy held out the bouquet in the glass vase. "Housewarming gift," she announced. "I'm so excited for you. Judging by the line I've seen outside all day, I'd say things are going well."

Ellie grinned. "It's amazing. Thank you for bringing the flowers. You need to add one of those flower-card holders with your company card so people can grab a card when they ask where the gorgeous arrangement came from," Ellie greeted her cheerfully.

Grinning at the smudge of flour decorating Ellie's round cheek, Daisy pantomimed wiping off her face. "Thanks! I'll remember to do that next time. I'm sure I'll be bringing over lots of flowers."

"I hope so. I love your arrangements."

Daisy leaned in to whisper confidentially, "You're killing it!"

"Cupcakes are the perfect treat. Small, but yummy. Portable. What else could you ask for?" Ellie laughed.

"Is Bear here by chance?" Daisy asked, feeling her cheeks warm.

"I knew it! He's been dancing around the kitchen like a Daddy who's found his Little. He *did*. Teddy found *you*!" Ellie celebrated, first carefully taking the vase from her friend and setting it down on the counter before rushing forward to wrap her arms around her friend. Happiness was contagious inside Little Cakes.

The two Littles jumped in a circle of glee, celebrating the new relationship. Everyone in the shop clapped to join the merriment, even though they had no clue why the women were happy.

"Littles," a deep voice behind them commented softly.

Laughing, Ellie and Daisy turned around to see Bear in his white apron with the Little Cakes logo.

"Bear, you should take a break! Just don't leave forever." Ellie turned conspiratorially back to face Daisy, pretending to cover her mouth as if Bear couldn't hear her. "He isn't really on the clock today, but he was going to show me the new lemon chiffon frosting he came up with. He's been calling it Daisy's Do," Ellie confided.

"Daisy's Do?" Daisy repeated with a wrinkled nose, glancing at Bear.

"It looks exactly like your hairdo would if I piled it on your head," Bear explained.

"Teddy!" Daisy protested, tugging on her braids. "I don't wear my hair in a high ponytail."

"You will when Daddy gives you a bath." Bear chuckled knowingly as Daisy felt her cheeks flame in reaction to the intimate act he suggested. He took Daisy's hand and led her into the workspace of the kitchen and out the backdoor.

"Little girl, I'm glad you came to visit. It was hard to leave you last night."

"Thank you for taking me home after I recovered. That shouldn't have bothered me so much," she said, trying to dismiss her fear.

"No way, Little girl," Bear corrected her. He sat down on the bench Ellie had placed behind the shop for employee breaks. Guiding Daisy, he helped her sit down on his lap. "You had a definite reason for reacting to that jerk. I'm sorry I wasn't there earlier to keep it from happening."

"I learned to yell. I think everyone suggested that."

"Good. I'm glad it's emblazoned in your mind. There are some people who enjoy being treated like Daddy Leo acted." He held up his hand to stop her next question. "He jumped over the most important step, though. When playing at a club with someone new, there has to be a negotiation of the scene. He shouldn't have assumed his actions turned you on. He was totally selfish—the exact opposite of what a Daddy should be."

"I don't really know what a Daddy should be like. I just know I didn't like the way Daddy Leo treated me. I go to Blaze to play with the other Littles. No one has seemed right for me."

"What time are you closing the shop?" Bear asked.

Surprised by the change in topic, Daisy looked at him, trying to follow his train of thought. "At the normal time, eight. Why?"

He sighed. "It looks like Ellie is going to sell most of the cupcakes we prepared for today. I need to work here tonight to help her restock. Tomorrow night I need to be at Blaze before you close. Will you come there when you get off work so we can talk about what you need from a Daddy?"

"Yes. You told me to save Friday night for you. I promise I will. And what are you looking for in a Little girl?" She forced herself to be brave.

Bear held her gaze with his. "From my side, it's fairly easy. I want you to be honest about what you want and need. I'll also require that you're romantically involved only with me."

"I don't want to have anyone else in my life," she whispered.

"That's good, Baby girl. Because I don't share what's mine."

Daisy nodded her head as those powerful words rang through her. He considered her his. Her lips tilted up in a pleased smile. "I like the sound of that. You know... That I'm yours."

Tightening the supporting arm Bear had wrapped around

her back, he pulled her in to place a soft kiss on her lips. When Daisy leaned forward eagerly, tilting her head to request another, the immense man accepted her invitation, deepening the kiss to taste the sweetness inside.

The desire that had kindled inside her as he held her on his lap flared hotter. Daisy wiggled closer, needing to feel his hard body against hers. Her nipples hardened as she felt herself becoming wet. Squirming on his lap, she discovered proof of his desire as his shaft stiffened against her. Confidence welled within her that this was not a game for Bear. He had picked her.

The fiery heat consumed them, making Daisy forget where they were. When Bear ripped his mouth from hers, breathing heavily, she objected with an escaping breathy protest, "Wait!"

Bear chuckled. "Did you forget where we are, Baby girl?" He rubbed his nose playfully against hers. "We're behind Little Cakes. I don't think you want Daddy to take things further where anyone could see us."

She cringed as she glanced around. He was right. "Sorry, Teddy."

He rubbed her back. "No reason to be sorry, Daisy. I enjoy kissing you. Will you do me a favor, Little one?"

She nodded. She'd do anything he asked. Was that reasonable at this stage in their relationship? They'd only officially declared their interest in each other four days ago, and they hadn't had much time to explore the spark yet, even though Bear seemed one-hundred percent certain she was his.

She didn't disagree. She'd lusted after the big man for a long time, too shy to put herself out there and take a risk. Or perhaps she'd been afraid of being shot down, which would have seriously hurt her feelings.

His hand slid up to her neck. "You're thinking awfully hard, Baby girl. Was my question too tough to answer?"

His eyes were dancing with laughter. "No, Teddy. I'll do any favor you ask me."

"Good. I want you to call me Daddy. Can you do that?"

She smiled and nodded. She could totally do that.

He lifted a brow. "Want to try it out?"

She giggled. "Daddy."

He hugged her close. "I like the sound of that." When he leaned back again, his expression was serious. "Hey, I forgot to tell you something. Did you see that the police arrested one of those thugs about an hour ago?"

She widened her eyes. "No. Where?"

"Here. The four of them came in and started harassing everyone. Three of them took off. The cops arrested the ring leader. They feel confident they will find the others soon. I thought you might have noticed the commotion out front."

She shook her head. How had she missed all that? "I guess that happened during my busy part of the day. There was a rush earlier."

Her mind raced as she remembered the flowers at the back door that morning. If those thugs had come back to harass her and pulled the flowers out of the trash, at least she now knew it wouldn't happen again, especially if the other three got picked up soon.

"You okay, Daisy?" he asked, his brow furrowed. "I'm sorry. I should have been more sensitive when I told you. You're shaking." He rubbed her arms.

She shook her head. "I'm fine. You really think the cops will find the other three?"

"Confident."

"Good." She took a deep breath and forced a smile. "I'm glad no one will have to worry about them anymore."

He slid his hand to the back of her head again and kissed her, not as deeply as he'd kissed her before, but enough that she was squirming and wanting more before he finished.

Daisy flinched when the back door opened. She lifted her gaze to see Lark stepping out back with a stuffed bag of trash in her hands.

Lark's eyes widened. "Oops. Sorry. Didn't mean to interrupt." She was fighting a grin, though.

Daisy was unsteady as Bear stood her on her feet and gave her one more sound kiss, obviously not caring they were being watched. He reached out and took the bag of trash from Lark. "Let me take this for you." He turned his attention back to Daisy. "Wait right here, Little girl. I'll walk you back to your shop."

"Okay." She would have called him *Daddy*. It was on the tip of her tongue. And she doubted Lark would care or think anything of it. After all, she was Ellie's best friend.

Daisy had no idea if Lark was Little or not, but she at least suspected the woman wasn't judgmental.

"The flowers you brought are beautiful," Lark said as Bear walked toward the dumpster. "That was very thoughtful of you."

"I wanted to bring something over to welcome Ellie to the strip mall on her opening day. I'm glad you like them."

"I bet Ellie will want to start a regular order with you. They really brighten up the room."

Daisy giggled. "With all those pretty cupcakes and the smell of delicious frosting, you don't need flowers to brighten up Little Cakes."

Lark smiled. "Still. Flowers make everything prettier," she declared.

"What are you girls giggling about?" Bear asked with a wink as he returned.

"Flowers," Daisy informed him. "They make life better."

"They sure do, Baby girl. I couldn't agree more." He wrapped a possessive arm around her and kissed her right on the mouth yet again. "I know a certain owner of a florist shop who also makes life better."

Daisy's cheeks heated as she melted against him.

"Uh, thanks for helping with the trash. See you later." Lark darted back inside before Daisy could respond.

"Let's get you back to your shop before I change my mind about PDA and really make you blush behind this bakery."

Chapter Five

Tarson kept a close eye on the entrance to Blaze, hardly straying away from the front for the first hour of his shift. He wasn't certain what time Daisy might arrive.

They'd exchanged several texts today when he'd finally gotten out of bed, but all he knew was she would be here after she closed the shop and stopped by her condo to change clothes.

When she finally came through the door, glancing around, his heart nearly stopped. He'd known she was his for almost a week, but every time he set his eyes on her, his certainty went up another notch.

He stood rooted to his spot, unable to move as she approached him. She had on the sweetest yellow party dress, yellow bows at the ends of her braids, and yellow ballet flats.

He also knew he'd made the perfect choices for her nursery because there was no doubt yellow was her favorite color.

She clasped her hands behind her back and swayed back and forth a bit as she shuffled closer. Her cheeks were flushed adorably as if she wasn't sure how he might respond to her.

When she stopped two feet shy of touching him, he

frowned. "That's it?" he teased. "You're not going to give Daddy a kiss? I've been waiting anxiously to see you all day."

She grinned and threw herself at him, jumping into his arms. Good thing he was prepared to catch her or the two of them might have taken a tumble backward.

Tarson grabbed her around the waist and hoisted her higher as she wrapped her small legs around him, her arms coming around his neck.

Damn, she felt good in his arms. She smelled good, too, like the floral shampoo she used or maybe her body soap. Not surprising. After all, flowers were her life.

When her lips came to his, all the tension he'd felt for the past few hours dissipated. He cupped her bottom with one hand and slid the other up her back, losing track of the world around him as he lost himself in the kiss.

Daisy was the sweetest Little girl he'd ever known. He'd looked for someone like her for years. Now that he had her in his arms and they weren't facing down scary thugs or fake Daddies or any other life challenges, he needed some time alone with her.

When he broke the kiss, still holding her in his arms, he guided her head to his shoulder and glanced around. He spotted Evan in moments. The backup Dungeon Master smiled knowingly and nodded toward the office.

Tarson was grateful Evan understood him well as he strode toward the office they shared, stepped inside, and shut the door. Without a word, he headed for the loveseat against the far wall and sat, his precious Little straddling his lap.

"I missed you, Baby girl."

Her cheeks pinkened. "I missed you too, Daddy."

He grinned wide. "Oh, I really like the sound of that."

She giggled.

"I like the sound of *that*, too." He kissed her again, needing to make up for all the hours he'd wished she were with him during the past week. He hoped she was in the same headspace as him and would be willing to take their relationship to another level starting now. Tonight.

He wanted her to go home with him. Sleep in the nursery he'd finished this afternoon. He wanted to spend as much time with her as possible and get to know everything about her.

"I love this dress, Baby girl," he murmured against her lips.

"Thank you. It's my favorite. I wanted to look pretty for you tonight."

"You always look pretty, Little one. I bet you would look smashing even in a gunnysack."

Another precious giggle. "That's just silly."

He slid his hands under her dress and up her bare back, pleased when he realized she wasn't wearing a bra. "Just stating the facts." He leaned in again, giving her another brief kiss because he couldn't help himself.

When he let his wide palms spread on her back so his thumbs grazed the sides of her breasts, her breath hitched. His voice was lower and deeper when he spoke again. "I bet you're even more beautiful naked."

The flush on her cheeks increased to a deep red on her pale skin and she lowered her gaze.

"Does that scare you, Baby girl? Am I taking things too fast?"

She shook her head quickly. "No, Daddy."

"Good. I promise I won't pressure you to take things further than you're ready for, Baby girl, but I would like to spend more time with you. We both have busy schedules, but how do you feel about sleeping at my house so I'll at least get to see you when neither of us is working?"

She grinned, thank goodness. "I'd like that, Daddy."

"Hey, I almost forgot. I wanted to tell you the police picked up the other three guys who terrorized your shop Sunday night. They were wanted for a number of crimes all over the state. They won't be out on bond anytime soon."

"Oh good. That makes me feel better. And for Ellie, too. I know she was also scared by them."

"Yes. Garrett was beside himself. We Daddies don't like our Littles in danger."

She leaned forward and kissed him again. "I feel safer now."

As she relaxed in his arms, he stroked the edges of her breasts again, making her arch her chest toward him and moan softly. When she didn't resist his touch, he eased his hands around to the front and cupped her small boobs in his palms.

She shuddered, her fingertips digging into his shoulders. Her blue eyes grew glassy, and she pressed her pussy against his growing erection. The only barrier between his slacks and her warmth was her panties.

He thumbed her nipples, watching her reaction closely every step of the way, loving how her body trembled and a whimper escaped her lips.

The precious Little squirmed against him so hard, he thought he might come in his pants. He loved how expressive and responsive she was to his touch, so he continued playing with her tight buds, flicking them and pinching them lightly.

"Daddy..." Her voice was soft and pleading.

"Would you let Daddy lie you back and make you feel good, Baby girl?" He wanted to see her come apart. He hadn't considered taking things this far before they got to his house later tonight, but he couldn't resist.

She nodded, her precious cheeks pinkening even further as she took her bottom lip between her teeth and bit down.

He wondered if her shyness with a touch of embarrassment was part of her Little side or if her adult persona also blushed at the mention of sex. He'd have to experiment and find out.

Scooting to one end of the loveseat, he lowered the back cushion down flat next to them and gently guided her onto her back. The cushion gave her enough height that her bottom was still on his lap while she lay flat beside him.

The best part was that her one leg was bent against his side, forcing her wide open. She was breathing heavily, watching his face, biting that lip.

With one hand on his biceps, she pushed her dress up above her panties. "Please, Daddy."

He loved that she was shy but still able to ask for what she wanted. And damn, her panties made his cock jump in his pants. White cotton with a yellow bow in front.

Tarson eased his hand up her inner thigh, pressing her outside leg wider, exposing her thoroughly. Her panties were soaked, and the moment he trailed his finger along the elastic edge between her legs, she moaned.

Those gorgeous blue eyes rolled back as he dragged the same finger over the top of the cotton, flicking the tip over her clit.

Her fingers dug into his arm. He wasn't sure she was aware of her grip, but he loved it. Her other hand was fisted in the flouncy material of her dress at her tummy.

Tarson palmed her pussy with one hand while he eased her other free of her dress and lifted it over her head. "Tuck your palm under your head, Baby girl."

She did as he instructed without hesitation. He'd never seen a prettier picture than the one before him. His Baby girl—and she was definitely his—flushed and eager and spread wide for him. Her pretty eyes glazed. Her pale skin splotchy with lust. Her pussy soaked. She was squirming against his lap, silently begging for more.

Tarson eased her dress up her body until he could see her breasts. He'd known she would be perfect, but she took his breath away. Her breasts were high and round, the nipples small and tight and so pink. He cupped one reverently, thumbing the tip again, loving the way she trembled.

He wanted to take all of her in, memorize this moment, this first time he would see his Baby girl come undone. His gaze slid from her eyes, to her button lips, to her sweet tits, to her belly, and down to her wet panties.

Even though she was blonde, he could tell she was shaved

bare, and he couldn't wait to see the rest of her, but he would save that for later, hopefully tonight.

For now, he would leave her panties on. Unless he ripped them off, he had no other choice in this position, and this moment was too gentle and sweet for him to tear the cotton off her body.

Nope. That one present would remain for later. He dragged his finger over the cotton several times until she writhed. "Daddy," she pleaded. Her voice was musical.

Tarson finally slid his fingers under the edge of her panties and drew them through her wet folds. Her bare skin teased him, making him harder than ever.

It was too soon to take her with his cock, but he knew he wouldn't be able to hold back for long. He needed the connection with her. He craved having her naked body against him, soft against hard, smooth against rough.

Thumbing her nipple with one hand, he eased his middle finger into her tight pussy, his gaze on her face.

Daisy lifted her hips clear off his thigh, her sexy body stiffening. "Oh, God. Please..."

He slid his finger almost out and then entered her again, deeper, as deep as he could reach. His thumb came to her clit and pressed down.

Daisy gasped, her mouth falling open. She stopped breathing and her entire body froze in time for a few precious seconds before her orgasm consumed her.

The tiny whimpers that escaped her lips were precious and he would look forward to swallowing them in the future, but for now, he could only watch her face. He couldn't possibly bend over far enough to kiss her, and he doubted she would be able to return the kiss anyway.

Her pussy was tight and gripped his finger hard with every pulse of her release. He wondered how long it had been since she'd had sex. He wasn't a small man. He would need to stretch her and take care with her the first time he entered her. The last thing he wanted would be to cause her pain.

When she started breathing normally again, he eased his finger out of her, circling her clit a few more times before he removed his hand from under the edge of her panties and brought his fingers to his mouth.

"Any reason I shouldn't taste your sweetness, Baby girl?"

Even while recovering from the pleasure he'd brought her, Daisy understood his question. "No, Daddy. I was tested after my last boyfriend a year ago."

"I'm glad you've taken care of yourself. I've been tested recently as well." He opened his mouth and lapped sensually at his fingers, carefully observing her reaction.

She blinked at him as he sucked her arousal from his middle finger. "Mmm. You taste so good, Baby girl."

Another precious flush.

"Thank you for letting Daddy make you feel good. I'll never forget this moment."

She pulled her hand from under her head and brought it to his cheek. "My turn?"

He chuckled. "Not this time, Baby girl."

She stuck out her bottom lip in a pout. "But that's not fair."

"Fair is a relative word, Little one." He reluctantly pulled her dress back over her distracting breasts before stroking her bottom lip with his thumb. "Surely you realize I'm the Daddy Dom in this relationship. Life won't always be fair, but I'll always take care of my Baby girl when she needs it."

He would not be removing his pants in this office inside Blaze so that their first time fully naked together would be someplace without total privacy.

After lifting her to sitting and settling her straddling his lap again, he palmed her hips under the dress. "I have to work for several hours, Baby girl. Will you be okay if I leave you in the daycare while I work?"

She nodded. "Yes, Daddy. I'll color with my friends like I always do."

He kissed her nose. "Good. Will you come home with me when I get done with my shift?"

She nodded again. "I'd like that, Daddy."

"Excellent. I have a surprise for you." He winked, giving her something to look forward to.

Her face lit up. "You do? At your house?"

"Uh-huh. I think you're going to like it. I've been working on it all week."

Her eyes widened adorably. "All week?"

"Yep. Ever since I came into your shop Sunday night. Remember, I told you then you were mine."

She swallowed. "I didn't let myself believe you were serious," she whispered.

"I know, but I'm hoping you're starting to believe me now. I meant it and I still do. I want you to be my Baby girl in every sense of the word."

She smiled, her head tipping shyly to one side. "I'd like that, Daddy. I can't wait until you get off work."

"I can't wait either, Baby girl." He stood and eased her to her feet. He hadn't let her yellow shoes hit the floor from the moment she'd jumped into his arms when she arrived, but he needed to be sure she was steady on her feet before he left her in the daycare.

He took her hand in his and led her from the office, knowing this was going to be the longest shift he'd ever worked at Blaze.

Chapter Six

"So, you and Teddy?" Ellie teased before yawning widely. "Oops!" The exhausted Little clapped a hand over her mouth before looking around the group apologetically.

"You have to be wiped out, Ellie. You've been baking for days!" Riley observed. She was off duty tonight and having fun being Little with the others in the daycare.

"But I don't want to interrupt your answer. You and Teddy?" she repeated, looking expectantly.

"We're together," Daisy admitted with a grin. "He asked me to call him Daddy."

"Wow! Congratulations!" Riley cheered with a big grin that sobered a bit as she continued, "I hope I find my Daddy someday."

"You will, Riley. Who knows, maybe it's someone close by?" Ellie suggested.

The trio glanced around at the Blaze members wandering outside the daycare. Milo Dante raised a hand to wave at them.

"Hi, Knot Master!" Daisy and Ellie chimed in together.

"Hi, Littles! What a pretty picture you all make together!"

"Have fun tying people up!" Ellie chirped.

"Thanks. I'm still looking for my perfect bunny," he added suggestively.

"Not me." Ellie shook her head emphatically.

"Me, neither." Daisy agreed with her friend that she wasn't drawn to that activity.

"Maybe, someday," Riley answered softly as she looked at the tabletop.

"Someday," Milo agreed, smiling at the woman with her head tilted down. He moved away after several long seconds of observation.

"Is he gone yet?" Riley whispered.

"Yes. Is something going on between you two?" Daisy probed. The tattooed, part-time Little was usually much more outgoing.

"Of course not." Riley dismissed the suggestion.

"I don't know. I think he was looking for you," Ellie suggested.

"He said 'Hi' to us, but looked at you the whole time, Riley," Daisy confirmed with an enthusiastic nod.

"He can't be interested in me. Milo has beautiful rope bunnies falling over him all the time," Riley murmured as if the idea were preposterous.

"Ahhh!" Ellie yawned and stretched her arms out in different directions.

"Time to go home, Little girl." Garrett's tone brooked no argument as the stern Daddy approached.

"Yes, Daddy," Ellie said, putting her crayon neatly in the basket and tearing the page from the coloring book.

"Look! I was almost finished." Ellie flapped the page at Garrett as she rushed to his side.

The handsome man accepted the picture and carefully held it up to peruse the sheet. "This is lovely, Little girl. I'd give it ten crayons."

"Yay!" Ellie cheered before dissolving into a jaw-cracking

yawn. She slipped her hand into Garrett's and with a friendly wave goodbye, followed him toward the exit.

"I don't know whether to hope her business slows down or keeps going at this pace. She's going to need more workers," Riley commented as they leaned back over their creations once again.

"They'll figure it out. Garrett's not going to let his Little work this hard for too long," Daisy observed.

"Speaking of working too hard," came another stern voice from over Daisy's head, "it's your bedtime as well, Daisy."

"Hi, Daddy," Daisy greeted him as she sprang to her feet and moved to stand in front of him. She couldn't believe how much she enjoyed calling him Daddy. Was this what the other Littles felt when they found their perfect match?

"Hi, Baby girl." He leaned down to press a kiss to her forehead before wrapping an arm around her waist to pull her close. "Do you want to bring your picture with us? I'd love to put it on my fridge."

"You don't have to do that," she protested as she moved to tear her page from the coloring book. "It's not very good."

"I love it. Want to know my favorite part?"

When she nodded, he continued, "I like the silvery stars in the night sky."

"I put those in myself," she said in awe.

"The perfect touch. Say goodnight to Riley," he prompted.

"Bye, Riley. I'll see you soon!"

"Definitely," the tattooed woman answered as she waved a crayon to say goodbye.

As Daisy's Daddy steered her through the lobby, she watched people note they were together. A couple called their congratulations. She thought her cheeks would crack from smiling so big as the dungeon master accepted their well wishes smoothly.

Once outside, he directed, "We'll go get your car. You can follow me home."

"I'm over there." Daisy pointed to the far end of the row.

They walked a few steps quietly before Daisy looked up at him to ask, "What's the surprise you have for me?"

"It won't be a surprise if I tell you, Baby girl."

He turned back toward her car. "Did you leave something on your windshield?"

"No..." Daisy sped up as she spotted something clumped in front of the driver's wheel. "They're daisies. That's sweet. Someone put my name flower on my car."

"I don't know if I like that, Daisy."

As they took the last few steps to end up next to the hood of the car, she noticed the flowers were wilted and soiled. Daisy traced a finger over the dirty, yellow center before something caught her attention. She pinched a tattered red ribbon between her fingers. There was no mistaking it. The same ribbon Blooms by Daisy had used for years.

"Oh, no!" she cried, dropping it and stepping back from the car to hide her face against Teddy's broad chest.

Immediately, he wrapped his arms around her and pulled her away from the car. "What's wrong? Talk to me, Baby girl."

"Are you sure those guys who broke in to my shop are still in jail?" she asked urgently, leaning away from the shelter of his body.

"As far as I know. What's going on?"

Words tumbled from her mouth in a waterfall of fright. "I found one of the bouquets that those guys destroyed Sunday night on the concrete in front of my back door on the day Little Cakes opened. You had put everything in the trash after the police took their pictures. I figured those jerks had come back to cause more problems and left me a warning."

"Baby girl..." Her Daddy started, but she interrupted him.

"I didn't tell anyone because they were caught, and I didn't think I had anything to worry about. But that ribbon," she pointed at the bedraggled piece wrapped around the wilted flowers. "That's the same ribbon I used for the wedding bouquet. It was missing from the flowers I found scattered on the ground."

"That means if they're still in jail, someone else is leaving you flowers."

"Yes," she wailed.

Bear pulled his phone from his back pocket and selected a number. "Detective Hazelton, this is Tarson Kirkwood. We met when four men invaded Little Cakes."

Daisy leaned forward, trying to hear what the police officer said in reply.

With a touch, Bear put his phone on speaker mode so she could listen. "I have Daisy from Blooms by Daisy here. I'm calling about those thugs who were terrorizing the strip mall. They had invaded her business and destroyed some floral arrangements last Sunday. She found one of the bouquets scattered back on the ground by her door yesterday morning but didn't report it because the men were later picked up. Are they still in jail?"

"Yes. They're being held until they appear in front of the judge. I think that's scheduled for tomorrow. I can call to double-check. Why? Has something else happened?" the detective probed.

"We just found more dead flowers on her windshield. They're wrapped with a grimy ribbon Daisy believes is the same from those bouquets."

"I know that's the same ribbon. I only use it on bouquets, and I haven't made any more since that day," Daisy rushed to add.

"I'm on duty tonight. Tell me your location and I'll be there. Leave everything alone until I get there," Detective Hazelton directed.

"We're at Blaze. It's a BDSM Club on the outskirts of town. I'll text you the address. If you can come in quietly, you'll scare a lot less people," Bear requested.

"I'll leave the flashing lights and siren alone." The detective chuckled before sobering to say, "Stay with her."

"I'm not leaving her side," Bear promised before hanging up.

The detective's last statement sent a shiver of fear through her. Daisy looked around to see if anyone lurked nearby. Were they watching to see her reaction? Was she still in danger?

"I'm not going to let anything happen to you, Baby girl." Her Daddy wrapped an arm around her waist and pulled her close before texting with his free hand.

With that task completed, he asked, "Why didn't you tell me about the flowers?"

"I really thought everything was okay after those men were arrested."

"Promise me you'll tell me anything that makes you even slightly nervous from now on. This isn't negotiable," he warned.

"I promise."

"Thank you, Baby girl."

The sound of an approaching car made them look down the drive. A police cruiser approached quietly. They watched the driver zero in on their location and pull behind Daisy's car.

"Tarson, Daisy," Detective Wyatt Hazelton greeted them as he exited the car.

"You remember my partner, Avery Reynolds," he mentioned to Bear.

"Hi. Thank you both for coming," Daisy chimed in. "I should have called before, but I thought the problem was solved and I didn't want to bother anyone."

"Always call. Better safe than sorry. Show me where you found the flowers today," Wyatt directed.

"We both noticed them as I walked Daisy to her car. They're under one windshield wiper," Bear explained as he backed up, guiding his Little with him.

"Did you touch anything?" Avery asked.

"I touched the ribbon without thinking. It's the kind that florist's order special for arrangements. That grade isn't usually available for commercial sale," Daisy explained. "We've had it in the shop for as long as I can remember."

She studied the officially dressed woman. Somehow, Daisy felt like she knew her—not in an official capacity, of course, but like she'd seen her somewhere before.

"Do you have a partner at your shop?" the policewoman probed, pulling Daisy from her thoughts as Wyatt pulled on gloves and moved to the front of the car.

"No. I have a couple of employees. I can't see either trying to scare me," Daisy rushed to defend her friends.

"Usually, it's someone you know—not just a random person," Avery shared.

"There's not a note or an overt threat. I'm going to take a few pictures to document this and seal the flowers in an evidence bag, just in case. It looks like someone's trying to scare you."

While Bear and Daisy watched, Wyatt completed those two things before asking. "Does anyone come to mind who might want to frighten you? A disgruntled employee or customer?"

"No. I have a great job. People love getting flowers, even on a sad occasion," Daisy assured him.

"I'll have the lab look these over but there's a backlog of cases. Unless there's an urgent threat, they'll put this on the back burner until they have some free time," Wyatt shared before he handed the bag to his partner.

As she walked to the trunk, Wyatt leaned in to ask privately, "May I ask the review process for joining the club? I'm new in the area and didn't know this existed here."

Daisy watched Bear pull a card from his wallet and hand it to the detective.

"As long as you're not trying to close us down, here's the website to apply. It will ask you for people who can vouch for you. Add my name if you're interested in adult play and can leave your officer status at the door. Membership is confidential and protected, of course."

"Of course. I can give you a contact at my last club to vouch for me as well," Wyatt assured him as he tucked the card into his wallet.

"You can add my name as well," Avery shared. "I'm a member but haven't been active since I lost my.... Well, that's not important."

"I thought you looked familiar!" Daisy rushed forward to hug the other woman.

"Is it safe for him to know you're Little?" Daisy whispered in her ear.

"I think so, but don't share that just yet," Avery answered, equally quietly.

Daisy stepped back and nodded. "I'm glad to see you. Could I have one of your cards? Just in case something else happens?"

Avery pulled out a slightly tattered card and handed it over. "Sorry. It's been mangled a few times in my pocket."

"Thanks," Daisy said, tucking it into the pocket of her poufy yellow dress before smoothing her hand over the fabric to make sure it was safely inside.

"Be alert to your surroundings. Call 911 or one of us if something or someone makes you uneasy. It's always smart to listen to what your intuition is telling you," Wyatt warned.

"I'm going to keep a close eye on her," Bear assured him.

"That's good. Listen to your Daddy." Wyatt directed the last part to Daisy.

"Oh!" she gasped as she realized Wyatt knew she was Little.

Her Daddy smoothed his hand over her back to reassure him. "Wyatt's safe, Baby girl."

Daisy nodded. She studied the ground under her yellow shoes before peeping up to ask Wyatt, "Are you a Daddy?"

"Yes," he answered simply.

His simple answer made Daisy peek at Avery. Her subtle

head shake clued Daisy in. The partners were simply that—work companions. Even though Wyatt had divulged his status as a Daddy, Avery wasn't ready to share her story.

The radio in the car squawked and both officers paused to listen.

"That's us. We'll need to head out. I'll be in touch," Wyatt stated as he and Avery headed back toward their squad car.

Chapter Seven

"Come in, Baby girl," her Daddy invited as he set her overnight bag inside the door.

Daisy could tell from his even deeper than normal voice that this was important to him. A warm feeling flared to life inside her. She liked knowing her presence in his house was a big deal—like she was something special and needed. After squeezing his hand, Daisy stepped into his home.

It was just as she had imagined her Daddy's home would be. Big, oversized furniture was arranged in a casual, homey style. The main room was huge with an open floor plan, allowing her to see into the kitchen and dining area as well.

"Your house is very welcoming," she complimented her Daddy before covering her mouth to yawn.

"Thank you, Baby girl. I'm glad you like it. You're so tired. It's past your bedtime."

"I don't really have a bedtime, Daddy."

"You do now. Little girls need lots of sleep. Come with me. Let me show you the surprise I put together just for you."

Curious, she followed him. They paused in the hallway for a minute as he opened a door and turned on the light. Stepping inside, Daisy clung to his hand as she looked around in amazement. *A nursery!*

"This is so beautiful. It's made for a fairy princess!" she breathed.

"Close. It was made for my floral princess," he corrected with a chuckle.

The room was painted a warm yellow. Daisy stroked her free hand over her dress as she realized he'd chosen a color very close to the one she wore. She crowded back, needing to be close to him as she looked around. Oversized baby furniture stood against different walls. The crib on the left and a changing table on the right. At the far end sat a wide rocker and a toy chest.

She turned her head to see the wall slightly behind her. A smaller chair sat facing away from the center of the room. A design spread across the walls on each side of the corner. Curious, Daisy walked towards it. The words, *Think Twice, I Love You, Be Good*, were scattered over the surfaces at eye level to someone sitting in that chair.

"What's this, Daddy?"

"That's your naughty corner."

"My naughty corner?" Daisy repeated, sure that she had heard him incorrectly.

"Yes."

"I'm not going to be naughty," she retorted.

"All Littles make bad choices from time to time. I don't think you'll be there often, but you will sit in that chair at some point."

"I don't think so," she corrected with a sniff. A glance at his face informed her that no matter how much she objected, her Daddy wasn't going to remove that chair. Daisy decided to change the subject.

"Do you think I could paint some flowers on the walls?"

"I think that would be incredible. You figure out what you need and we'll make a list and go get the paint and brushes.

We'll block out time on our schedules to paint. For now, it's time for my Little girl to be in bed."

Daisy turned to look at the crib. Its beautifully curved white wooden slats were graceful and inviting. It looked like a bed designed with care for someone loved. "I don't want to mess it up," she suggested.

"Your crib won't be happy without a Little to take care of. That's what it has been designed to do. Without someone nestled inside, it loses its worth," Teddy answered.

"But what if it isn't supposed to be mine?" Daisy whispered, looking longingly at the crib.

"Do you trust me, Baby girl?"

"Y... Yes." She didn't understand her stuttered answer. There was no one she trusted more than her Daddy. From the beginning, when she had met him at Blaze, she'd trusted the enormous dungeon master. He kept everyone safe.

As if reading her thoughts, her Daddy commented, "Give yourself time to adjust. There's no pressure."

Daisy rushed forward to wrap her arms around his waist. She clung to his body, allowing his strength to steady her. When he stroked her back, she closed her eyes and whispered, "I so want this to be real."

"Do I feel real to you?" he gently asked.

Tightening her arms around him, she whispered, "Yes."

"You feel real to me," he shared. "I think your mind needs to catch up with your heart. Sometimes, Little girls overthink things."

She nodded against his broad chest. That's exactly what she always did—turn things over in her mind and think about them repeatedly. Daisy didn't quite know how to stop, but she tried creating a door in her brain and shoving all her worries inside. Slamming that barrier shut, she relaxed against her Daddy.

"That's it, Baby girl."

They stood silently wrapped in each other's arms for several minutes. When Teddy dropped a kiss on the top of her head, she lifted her lips to invite another. To her delight, he obliged. Warm heat built in her tummy as his mouth slowly explored hers.

Daisy jolted forward when a quick swat landed on her bottom. She jerked her lips away from his in surprise. "What...?"

"That's for distracting your Daddy. It's bedtime, Baby girl. Let's get you clean. Do you like showers or baths?"

"Showers when I'm in a hurry and baths when I have lots of time."

"Perfect. Bath tomorrow when we get started earlier. Shower tonight," he announced as he stepped away from her to take her hand.

Following his massive form out of the nursery, Daisy looked back one more time to take in the wonder of the special room. She hated to leave it. Feeling silly that a room could be so important, Daisy followed Daddy into the master bedroom through a connecting door.

His bedroom décor was dark and rich. She realized that a man who slept frequently during the day would need to control the sunlight that invaded. Daisy loved the deep burgundy curtains that looked like they were made of soft velvet. The walls were painted a deep brown that matched the dappled carpet under her feet. The bedding combined all the colors in a muted, abstract design to pull everything together.

She giggled as they walked through slowly when she noted her Daddy only had two fluffy pillows on his bed. Daddies obviously didn't follow the fashionable trend of displaying a mound of decorative cushions.

As they stepped onto the tiled floor of the large bathroom, she resisted slightly. *Am I going to take a shower in here? Is he joining me?* She watched her Daddy reach into the large walk-in shower to turn on the water.

"I want it to be warm for you," he explained, walking back

to stand in front of her. "Come on, Baby girl. Let's get you undressed."

"Arms up," he directed as he pulled her pretty dress over her head.

Automatically, she lifted her hands toward the sky. Exposed to his eyes, Daisy could feel her nipples harden.

His hands slid to the sides of her breasts. "So pretty," he said reverently.

Daisy fought her own insecurities as her Daddy complimented her. *He likes me just as I am.* His light kiss on her forehead reassured her, making her smile.

"That's my good girl. Now, your panties." Quickly, he slid her underwear over her hips and down to her ankles.

"Step out of your shoes, Baby girl," Daddy directed as he set her clothing on the vanity.

Within seconds, Daisy stood nude in front of him. She kept herself from shielding her body from his view, hoping she would be enough for him. He caressed her cheek before threading his fingers through her hair to cup the back of her head.

"Never did I dream I would be lucky enough to find a Little girl who is beautiful inside and out. I am a very lucky Daddy. Now, into the shower so you don't get cold. I'll join you in a few seconds," he said, stepping back to whip his T-shirt over his head.

Captivated by the chiseled muscles in his torso, Daisy took a step toward him instead of the shower. She raised a hand to touch his deep brown skin.

"In the shower, Baby girl." Her Daddy pointed behind her as he stepped back.

Daisy froze and lifted her gaze to study his face. She couldn't touch him? After watching him shake his head at her, Daisy turned and walked toward the shower as she looked at him over her shoulder for confirmation that she was doing what he wanted. His stern look faded to be replaced with a pleased expression. Her lips curved up at the corners. *I like making him happy.*

She stepped onto the tiled floor and turned the corner leading into the large shower. Pausing where she could peek around the corner back at him, Daisy watched him unfasten his jeans and push them off his hips. Automatically, her mouth opened in a rounded "Oh!"

She must have made some slight sound because he looked up. When their gazes meshed, she quickly scooted forward out of his sight and into the warm water. Feeling her cheeks heat with embarrassment for being caught ogling him, Daisy closed her eyes and put her face into the stream of liquid.

His body heat warned her that he now stood in the shower with her. Daisy wiped the water from her eyes and looked over one shoulder. He was there. Naked and incredibly hot.

Pulled magnetically toward his fit body, Daisy tried not to be obvious as she memorized his form. His thick erection pointing proudly toward his navel captured her attention. At the sound of him clearing his throat, she ripped her gaze up to meet his.

"What big eyes you have, Baby girl."

"That's never going to fit," tumbled from her lips.

"It will fit," he assured her with a soft smile.

When she shook her head, her gaze lowered back to the thick shaft. His fingers, gentle under her chin, lifted her head until his dark eyes looked into Daisy's. "We'll fit perfectly together when it's time for us to join our bodies. Tonight is not the night. You're tired and need to be in bed."

"But..." Her voice trailed off as she attempted to look down again.

His hand held her chin in place. "You trust me," he reminded her.

Instantly, she tried to nod her head, but his hold negated that. Daisy whispered, "Yes."

"I won't hurt you, Baby girl. I plan to make you scream with pleasure."

Her imagination exploded into visual images of their bodies moving together. She nodded, not realizing he had released her. Her Daddy swept silky lavender soap over her skin. Daisy shivered at the feel of his slightly roughened fingers moving over her body.

He lingered here and there. Never long enough to push her arousal into overdrive, he simply showed her how much he appreciated her curves. Her Daddy turned her gently into the spray of water to rinse away the suds. Kneeling at her feet, he washed from her toes to the tops of her thighs before rising to stand behind her. After wrapping one arm around her waist to hold Daisy steady against his body, Teddy dipped his fingertips into her pink folds to clean between her thighs.

Daisy leaned back against him, widening her legs to invite his touch. Even soaked by the cascading water, his fingers slid through the slick juices gathered there.

"Let Daddy make you feel good," he suggested.

Nodding, she would have agreed to anything he said. Daddy explored her body, tracing the sensitive opening before gliding two fingers deep into her body. He held them in place as her body clenched to maintain his touch inside her. Slowly, he stroked in and out of her body, circling her clit before tapping on it.

Heat built inside her body. The erotic sight of him caressing her body weakened her legs, making her lean against him for stability. Daisy fluttered her eyelids closed to concentrate on the sensations before forcing them back open to watch. With a cry, she came—shattered by his skilled touch. She melted against his chest.

"That's my pretty Baby girl. I love to feel you come on my fingers. Soon, I'll be buried deep inside you."

"Please," she begged in a hoarse whisper.

He pressed hot kisses against her neck, sending shivers

through her body. "Soon," he promised, before turning off the water with a snap of his wrist that revealed his impatience as well.

Marveling at his iron-clad control, Daisy loved his tender care as he dried her body carefully with a fluffy towel. Suddenly completely exhausted, she struggled to keep her eyes open as he wrapped a towel around her body before encircling his waist with another. She allowed him to guide her out of the bathroom and into the large bedroom.

"You'll have to wear one of my T-shirts until your nighties arrive." Teddy opened a drawer and selected a blue shirt that matched her eyes. He quickly draped it over her head and gently tugged it into place.

Lifting her into his arms, he carried her into the nursery. Her Daddy walked directly to the crib. He tucked her into the crib, pulling the soft comforter up to her chin.

"Sleep well, Baby girl. I'm right next door if you need me." He leaned into press a soft kiss to her lips. "Close your eyes, Daisy."

Unable to resist the invitation of the cozy bedding, she settled on her side and followed his directions. Daisy felt his presence as he stood next to the crib. Comforted by his closeness, she drifted off to sleep.

Standing next to her crib, Tarson memorized the sight of his Little girl. Her faint sleepy sounds etched themselves in his heart. He knew he would do anything and everything to keep her safe and happy.

With pure determination, he forced himself away from his vigil after her breath settled into a regular pattern. Retracing his steps, Tarson stopped at the vanity to pick up her panties. He lifted the scrap of lace to his nose and inhaled before washing the garment in the sink. Draping the damp fabric over the towel rack, he took a second to hang up her pretty dress in his closet.

With all his tasks done, Tarson hung up his towel and flipped the water back on in the shower. The scent of lavender soap made him picture Daisy as he'd washed her. Sticking his face under the water flow, he tried to control his resurging passion.

His hand grasped his cock and he groaned at the sensitivity. "I'm not going to die before I make her mine. Soon," he promised himself as he yanked his fist down his erection. His eyes closed to remember the feel of her silken skin flushed with her arousal. Daisy was perfect. She was his.

With a muffled shout, he came against the tiled wall. Tarson braced his arm against the wall to recover. When his heartrate slowed, he forced himself to finish his shower. Drying his skin roughly, he walked to his bed and threw back the covers.

"No way," he muttered aloud before turning to pull on lounge pants and pacing back into the nursery. Tarson needed to stay with his Little girl. He lifted the large rocker and pulled it next to the crib. Settling where he could see her, Tarson closed his eyes. If she needed him, he wanted to be close.

Chapter Eight

Daisy woke up slowly. She was so comfortable. Why did her bed seem so much softer, the covers fluffier than usual? As she blinked awake, she gasped, her eyes shooting wide open. *This isn't my bed.*

She pushed to sitting, her heart racing as she scanned the room. It took only a second to remember where she was, especially when Daddy popped up from the rocking chair next to her and hovered over her immediately.

"Hey there, Baby girl. Did you wake up confused?" He set a hand on her tummy as she dropped back onto the soft mattress.

"Yes, Daddy." She glanced around the room. The lighting was dim. "What time is it?"

"It's early. Six o'clock. What time do you need to be at your shop today?" He rubbed her belly through the covers.

"Ten."

"Plenty of time then. Do you want to go back to sleep for a while?"

She shook her head. "No. I'm not tired anymore. Maybe I could check out some of the toys in the toy box?" she asked hopefully. It would be a treat to have a few hours to chill before heading to work. A few hours to be in her Little space without adult responsibilities.

Saturday mornings were usually hectic because if she were home, she would do a load of laundry, clean the bathrooms, and put something in the crockpot. Not being in her own home this morning made her feel like she could forgo her usual chores.

Daddy lowered the side of the crib and pulled her covers back. When cool air hit her pussy, she realized her shirt had ridden up, leaving her exposed. Instinct caused her to reach down and tug Daddy's T-shirt over her nudity.

Daddy's hand came to hers, stopping her before she managed to pull the soft cotton far enough to conceal herself. "No need to cover yourself when you're with Daddy, Baby girl. I've seen every inch of you, and I intend to do so often."

Her face heated and she pursed her lips while she nodded. She shifted her attention to his broad chest. He wasn't wearing a shirt. And when she glanced lower, she saw that his sleep pants were low on his hips and tented in the front.

She remembered how big he was from last night. With his large palm wrapped around her fingers against her belly, her pussy exposed, and his chest so inviting, wetness pooled between her legs, making her feel restless.

He'd given her an amazing orgasm last night, but he hadn't let her touch him, nor had they had sex. Would he have sex with her now?

"Your eyes are very big this morning, Baby girl. Does it arouse you to wake up in your crib with your bottom exposed?"

She jerked her attention to his face, licking her lips. "You're very sexy, Daddy." She flushed as the words left her lips.

He grinned. "I'm glad you're attracted to me, but we need to take care of a few things this morning before we head down that path."

"What things?" she asked curiously.

"I bet you're hungry, and I bet you need to go potty." He lifted a brow.

She squirmed as he applied slight pressure to her tummy, reminding her she indeed needed to use the bathroom. She'd been half asleep when he put her in the crib last night, but she was a bit surprised now that he hadn't diapered her last night.

She'd seen the stacks of diapers under the changing table. They'd been impossible to miss. She'd never worn a diaper before when spending time in her Little space. It hadn't seemed like something she wanted to do alone in her condo.

Daisy was aware that some Littles liked to spend time in a very young space, but the opportunity had never presented itself to her. She'd sometimes fantasized about the idea, but the prospect of buying diapers, putting them on herself, and then changing them had never appealed to her.

Maybe Daddy would be interested in letting her explore that side of herself. Surely he wasn't opposed or he wouldn't have bought all those diapers she'd seen.

Her tummy grumbled and the pressure in her bladder intensified at the same time, reminding her he'd asked her a question. "Both, Daddy. I need to pee and I'm hungry. I don't usually eat breakfast in the mornings though. I usually just make a smoothie. My tummy gets upset if I eat too much so early. Plus, I'm usually in a hurry."

He smiled. "I can definitely make you a smoothie." He released her hand and bent down to lift her into his arms.

She gasped softly as she wrapped her legs around him, her bare pussy against his hip.

He turned toward the changing table. "Would you like to use the potty in the bathroom or would you like Daddy to put a diaper on you?"

She swallowed and met his gaze. "I've never worn a diaper, but I'd like to try. Would that be okay? You don't mind?"

He tickled her under her chin as he carried her to the changing table and laid her on her back. "Of course I don't mind, Baby girl. I wouldn't have a changing table and diapers if I didn't want you to use them."

When he pushed her T-shirt up and then pulled a strap across her waist, she started to tremble. This was really happening. Could she pee in a diaper? She wasn't sure.

Daddy reached below her to grab something from the shelf and held it up in front of her.

She grinned widely as she saw the pretty bear. He had a halo of daisies around his head and a yellow shirt on.

"How about if you hold this fellow while I diaper you?"

She took him from Daddy and hugged him against her chest. "What's his name?"

"I don't know. He didn't tell me. I think he was waiting for you to name him." Daddy winked as he lifted her legs and slid the crinkly diaper under her bottom. "Let's see... What's your favorite cupcake flavor?"

"Lemon Chiffon, of course," she responded indignantly. *Duh.*

Daddy chuckled as he lifted the front of the diaper up around her waist. "My bad. I should have guessed. Then how about you name him Lemmy?"

Her eyes widened and her mouth dropped open in horror. "That would hurt my favorite stuffie's feelings. His name is already Lemmy."

Daddy chuckled. "You have a stuffie at home named Lemmy?"

"Yes."

"Is he a bear?"

"Of course not, silly. He's a lemon."

Daddy laughed harder as he closed the diaper and then unfastened her from the table to lift her into his arms. He set her on the floor in front of him and squatted down to meet her gaze at eye level, his hands on her biceps.

"My apologies to the real Lemmy. I hope he won't be offended. We'll have to come up with another name for this fellow then." Daddy patted the bear on the head.

Daisy giggled. "Don't be silly, Daddy. Lemmy can't be mad.

He didn't hear you. He's at my condo." She lowered her voice to a whisper. "But maybe we just won't tell him about your blunder so the two of you won't start off on the wrong foot."

Daddy laughed harder. "Good plan, Baby girl. I'm going to go fix you a smoothie. You can explore the nursery while I'm gone, but be careful waddling around in your diaper. You won't be very steady this first time. It takes some getting used to."

"Yes, Sir." She glanced down, squeezing the new teddy bear against her chest as she took in her padded bottom. A wave of apprehension filled her. She wasn't certain she could actually use the diaper, and she was slightly embarrassed for suggesting it.

Daddy kissed her forehead and left her alone in the nursery. As soon as he was gone, she took her first tentative steps. It was awkward, but she also felt oddly at home. Peaceful.

Was it reasonable that sleeping over at her new Daddy's house, and then wearing a diaper on her first morning, would make her feel like she belonged?

After making her way to the toy box, she leaned over the edge and smiled. It was filled with dolls and other stuffies. She still held the bear against her chest as if he were a lifeline.

She also needed to potty. Badly. Gripping the edge of the toy box, she closed her eyes, willing her body to relax. She could do this. She knew Daddy wouldn't judge her for using a diaper. He wanted her to. He'd encouraged her to. Obviously, if he didn't want to deal with the mess of cleaning her up, he wouldn't have bought the diapers and put one on her.

She kept telling herself this, the reminder slowly sinking in until she finally managed to release her bladder.

The heavy bulk between her legs made her shiver. She felt far more Little than she had in her life. This was a huge step. She wasn't sure she would always want to be this Little, but maybe sometimes. She hoped Daddy didn't think she would wear diapers all the time. That would never work. Especially when she was at her flower shop.

She was so deep in thought she didn't hear Daddy approaching behind her until he set a hand on her shoulder. "Feel better, Baby girl? I'm proud of you."

She nodded, not able to voice how she felt. She wasn't entirely certain. Her emotions were all over the place.

Daddy swept her off her feet and gently placed her back on the changing table. This time, after he strapped her down, he took a bit longer caring for her, removing the soaked diaper before cleaning her folds with a warm wipe.

Daisy held her breath as he stroked her clit several times with the thin cloth, and she let out a little gasp when he reached lower to clean her butt crack, paying special attention to the tight ring of muscles. She hoped he didn't expect her to go number two in the diaper. She wasn't ready for that.

"Is it okay if I put another diaper on you, Baby girl?" he asked gently. "We'll put your big girl clothes on when it's time for you to leave for work, okay?"

She nodded, nuzzling the yellow ribbon of her bear as Daddy continued wiping her. She whimpered when he found her clit.

"Does that feel good, Baby girl?"

She nodded and licked her lips. "When will you have sex with me?"

He smiled as he closed her fresh diaper. "Let's see how you feel after we get a smoothie in you, okay? I know you're hungry."

After unfastening her from the changing table, Daddy lifted her into his arms, hugging her close to his chest. He'd put a T-shirt on while he'd been gone, which was kind of disappointing. She'd enjoyed looking at his bare chest.

"I'm so very glad you're here, Baby girl," he whispered in her ear as he carried her to the oversized rocking chair and sat with her in his lap.

The way he cradled her in his arms felt so comforting. She couldn't remember when she'd last felt this content. She'd been on her own for a long time. Ever since her parents had moved to Florida last year, she'd been too busy to be in any sort of relationship. Her down time had mostly been spent unwinding at Blaze.

With the exception of the thugs who had tried to terrorize her in her shop, things had settled down for her recently. Maybe she could finally let herself have a personal life. Maybe Bear was just the man to make that happen.

She smiled up at him. "I'm glad I'm here, too, Daddy."

He hugged her against his chest again as if he couldn't quite get enough of her, and she liked it. When he released his tight grip again, he leaned her back in his arms like an infant.

She was surprised and a bit uncertain as he reached over to pick something up from the floor and then held a bottle to her lips. He must have set it there when he came into the room before she noticed him. "A bottle, Daddy?"

"Yep. Your smoothie. I hope you won't mind sitting in my lap and letting me feed you sometimes. Daddies enjoy holding their Little girls close while they drink their bottles."

She stared at the nipple for a moment. Like the diaper, drinking from a bottle had also been a fantasy of hers. Not one she'd ever expected to fulfill. She could have purchased some bottles and filled them herself, but she'd never wanted to be the one to hold them. That hadn't been her vision. *This* had been her vision. A Daddy feeding her himself. Was she dreaming, or was she the luckiest Little girl alive?

Daddy stroked her lips with the nipple. "Try it for me, Baby girl. I think you'll like it."

She opened her mouth and let him slip the nipple inside. She didn't need to try it to know she would like it. She was certain she would love it. In fact, she squirmed in his lap the moment she wrapped her lips around the rubber nipple. Her pussy clenched and butterflies danced in her tummy.

As she took the first suck of delicious smoothie and swallowed it, she drew her knees up and tried to squeeze her thighs together. It wasn't possible around the bulk of the diaper, and the need for pressure against her pussy was intense enough that her hand flew down between her legs to press against the padding.

Daddy chuckled as he wrapped his fingers around her wrist and drew her hand to her side. "I think my Baby girl likes taking a bottle for Daddy."

Her face heated as she realized he knew she was turned on by being coddled like this. She arched her chest, rubbing her breasts against his forearm as she took another long suck from the bottle.

Daddy lifted his arm out of her reach, tipping the bottle up so she couldn't get purchase on anything. "Bottle first, Baby girl, and then Daddy will take care of the ache."

She should have been embarrassed, but he seemed so pleased, she tried not to let her arousal bother her. It wasn't as if she could keep it a secret from him. She was failing miserably.

Every time she wiggled, she was reminded of the fact that she was diapered. Every time she took another drink of smoothie, she was reminded she was being fed from a bottle.

She closed her eyes as she continued sucking, overwhelmed with emotion. This was what she'd dreamed of for so long. She'd always hoped to one day find a Daddy, someone she could make a life with, but she'd never dared hope for an arrangement that would come anywhere close to what she'd pictured as the perfect nurturing environment.

When the bottle was empty, Daddy set it back on the floor and flattened his palm on her tummy over the T-shirt. He held her gaze. "I have a question, Baby girl. Is this what you fantasize about when you masturbate? A Daddy who takes care of your every need?"

Heat rose in her cheeks once again. How embarrassing. She turned her head to bury her face in his chest.

He patted her diapered bottom as she rolled toward him. "No reason to be embarrassed, Daisy. It pleases me greatly to find out you enjoy me taking care of you the way I've longed for. I just want to make sure you get what you need out of our relationship. If spending time in a very young space is titillating to you, I feel like the luckiest Daddy alive."

She set her palm on his chest and ran it up around his neck as she inhaled his scent, hoping he didn't expect her to answer.

When Daddy slid his hand under her T-shirt and eased it up to cup her breast, she arched into him. He found her nipple and thumbed it next, making her whimper.

Wetness gathered between her legs, and she had no way to ease the need since he was still gripping her other wrist with his fingers.

"Do you want Daddy to take you to his bed, Baby girl?"

She nodded against him, moaning as he gave her nipple a pinch. She was beyond pleased when he stood and carried her through the connecting door into his bedroom.

This was really happening.

Chapter Nine

Daisy wrapped her legs around Daddy's waist tightly, not wanting to release her grip when he eased her onto his bed. His smile sent shivers through her body as he pushed the T-shirt up her body and over her head.

His hands came to the tabs on her diaper next and he chuckled. "You'll have to let Daddy go if you want me to remove this diaper and take my clothes off, Baby girl."

She reluctantly untangled her ankles and let her knees fall open, watching Daddy's strong features as he unfastened her diaper.

Daisy had never felt this open with a man before. Open enough to keep her knees spread wide while he stared at her. She knew she was wet and her folds were probably swollen, both from craving contact for such a long time and from him cleaning her skin.

Her gaze slid to his chest as he drew his shirt over his head, then lower to his cock as he dropped his sleep pants to the floor. She'd seen him last night, but he hadn't let her touch.

Daisy was torn between needing him inside her and wanting to hold him in her hands and taste him. The second desire won out, and she scrambled to drop off the side of the bed and stand before him.

"Where're you going, Baby girl?" he asked as he fisted his shaft and ran his hand from the base to the tip.

She leaned her head back to look up at him. "May I touch you this morning, Daddy?" she asked, hoping to sound so sweet that he couldn't turn her down.

He lifted a brow skeptically. "You look rather mischievous. You may explore for a minute, Baby girl, but I want to come inside you, not on your hand or in your mouth."

"Yes, Sir." She took a step forward and reached for the bobbing length, letting her fingers dance up and down the shaft, grinning when he moaned.

Daddy threaded one hand in her hair. "You drive me crazy, Daisy."

Good. It made her feel powerful to know she affected him as much as he did her.

He was tall enough that she only needed to bend slightly to flick her tongue over the tip of his cock. The salty taste made her want more of him, but he gave her hair a slight tug, stopping her.

"That's all I can take for now, Baby girl. You can suck me into your mouth another time. It's been a long time since I've had a Little girl. I'm not going to last long. Can you be a good girl and climb up into the middle of the bed, Little one?"

She reluctantly released him. "Okay, Daddy." She turned to climb back onto his high mattress, giggling when his hands came to her hips to give her a boost. "Like this?" she teased as she reached the middle, still on all fours, her butt facing him.

He slid up behind her, his hands on her hips again. "Funny girl. Do you think I'm not tempted to take you from behind? Is that what you want?"

She pursed her lips and thought about her actions. The truth was, this was exactly what she wanted. Another of her fantasies. To be pressed into the mattress on her tummy while her Daddy slid between her legs and claimed her.

As if he read her mind or simply judged her needs from her hesitation, his hand slid to the small of her back. "Drop onto your chest, Baby girl. Keep your knees bent and spread wide. Bottom in the air."

She shuddered as she did as he told her while he released her to reach toward the nightstand. She shuddered again when she heard the sound of a condom wrapper opening.

Finally.

The moment he was between her knees, she released a breath she hadn't known she was holding. Maybe it should have felt awkward to have her bottom so blatantly exposed to Bear's view, practically begging him to take her doggy style, but this wasn't just Bear—the sexy dungeon master who'd made her pussy weep for as long as she'd known him. This was her Daddy, the man who'd come to her rescue when she'd needed him—more than once now.

This was Daddy, the man who'd put in a yellow nursery for her and checked off so many of her list of fantasies in the last twelve hours alone.

Daddy set one hand on the small of her back and brought the other between her legs. The moment he touched her folds, she moaned. "Please, Daddy. I need you."

"I know, Baby girl, but I want you to come first. Let Daddy make you feel good and then I'll fill you up with my cock."

She fisted her hands in the blankets at the sides of her head as she wiggled her butt.

"My needy Little girl is so wet for Daddy. Wearing the diaper and taking the bottle for Daddy made you very horny, didn't it, Baby girl?"

She whimpered. He was right, and he knew it. She wouldn't try to deny it. He'd seen the evidence.

When he thrust two fingers into her, she lifted her head and cried out. "Daddy!"

He found her clit, stroking it hard as he held his fingers deep inside her. "Come around Daddy's fingers, Daisy. You're so close already. I've barely touched you. Do you know how hard that makes my cock?"

She couldn't focus any longer. Not on anything but the building pressure and the need to come. Seconds later, her orgasm took over, making her arch her neck while she groaned out her release.

Her legs were shaking and her pussy pulsing as his fingers disappeared. "Daddy..." she begged.

She didn't have to wait any longer though. Daddy nudged her knees out so she flattened onto the mattress. He dropped down on top of her, lined his cock up with her entrance, and pressed slowly into her tight body. Daisy focused on relaxing her muscles to allow him to glide in fully. Several times he stopped and pulled out slightly to allow her to recover before sliding deeper. Finally, he was inside her completely.

All the breath left her lungs as the weight of Daddy's body surrounded her. His hands came to her fists, holding her tight. His lips came to her ear. "Is this what you dreamed of, Baby girl?"

"Yes, Daddy. So much," she whispered.

"Good girl. You feel so good around Daddy's cock. So very good." He kissed her temple as he eased out and thrust back into her.

Every nerve ending in her channel pulsed around his length as if dozens of tiny orgasms fluttered inside her. She'd never experienced anything this amazing. Never dreamed it was possible.

This kind of sex was the thing of fantasies, not reality. It was hard to believe it was really happening.

After a few more languid thrusts, Daddy whispered in her ear again. "Can I turn you over, Baby girl? I want to look into your eyes when I come inside you."

"Yes, Daddy."

She was shaking like a rag doll as he pulled out and flipped her onto her back. "Knees bent, legs wide, Baby girl."

She obeyed his command immediately, loving the way he looked at her. His sheathed cock was bigger than earlier, straining against the condom.

He lowered between her legs, threaded their fingers together, and held her hands above her head. The restraint made her arousal shoot back to a ten, and when his chest brushed against her nipples, she moaned.

"Such a pretty girl." He thrust into her, taking her breath away yet again. "Fast or slow, Daisy?"

"Fast, please, Daddy."

His lips descended onto hers, forcing her attention to shift to their kiss for a moment as his tongue slipped inside to toy with hers.

She was overwhelmed with sensations, too many to count, and she gasped in his mouth when he pulled almost out and thrust back in hard.

Her vision blurred and she couldn't continue kissing him. She didn't have the brain cells to tell her lips to move.

He didn't mind though. He released her mouth to stare down at her while he thrust again. Harder. Faster. Deeper.

Another orgasm slammed into her without warning, taking her by surprise as her pussy gripped his cock.

He must have liked it too, because seconds later, he groaned out his own release on top of hers. Their mutual unintelligible noises filled the air.

For a long time, Daddy continued to hold her tight, his chest hovering close enough to make her feel surrounded without crushing her.

Eventually, he eased out, leaving her empty and so sated.

"Don't move, Baby girl," he whispered. "Be right back."

He disappeared. There was no chance of her moving, possibly ever again.

When he returned, he set a wet cloth between her legs and

gently wiped her pussy and thighs. She was too limp to argue or care as he lifted her butt off the mattress and slid another diaper under her. Without protest, she threaded her arms through the oversized T-shirt once again, enjoying the sensation of the soft cotton wrapped around her.

She couldn't keep her eyes open. She was overwhelmed. As reality slipped back in, she began to fret.

Daddy pulled the covers back, tugging them from underneath her before settling her in the middle of his bed and tucking her in.

Daisy curled onto her side and brought her thumb to her mouth, needing the comfort of being incredibly Little while she processed what was happening.

She whimpered when Daddy gently tugged her hand away from her mouth, but settled again when he replaced it with what she assumed was a pacifier. A second later, he tucked her teddy bear in her arms.

The bed dipped as he curled around her with an arm wrapped over Daisy's body to hold her close to him. She snuggled back closer to him and closed her eyes as she relaxed against him.

"Such a good Baby girl," he complimented. His hand smoothed over her tummy, soothing her.

His lips pressed against her temple. "Nap for a bit, Baby girl. You don't have to be at the store for another few hours. Daddy will wake you in a while."

She was exhausted, but her mind was racing with so many thoughts and concerns. Not only had her Daddy explored her body with skill and sensitivity, but he'd also anticipated exactly what she'd needed. Had he known? Was that why he'd tucked her in and given her a pacifier?

This entire situation was far too good to be true. Bear was fulfilling all her wildest dreams. Could something like this last? Could it be real and forever?

She wouldn't let herself hope for something so perfect. It would devastate her if it didn't work out. She'd known Bear for a while, but the idea of him being *her* Daddy was relatively new. She'd barely let herself believe it was true, and now he'd taken her places that had previously only existed in her dreams.

She needed to guard her heart. Maybe it was too soon for her to believe this could last forever. Plus, she wasn't sure Bear would want her to be as Little as she found herself craving.

Sure, he'd been the one to provide her with the bottle, diapers, crib, and pacifier. But had he meant for her to use those things all the time? Maybe he pictured her sleeping in that crib, wearing a diaper, and taking a bottle only occasionally. Like a scene.

She enjoyed being his Baby girl so much she didn't want it to end. But that wasn't realistic for so many reasons. For one, she had to work. She had to put on her adult clothes, flip a switch in her mind, and be a professional about ten hours a day.

Also, playing in Little space this young was intense. As much as she craved it, it might be too overwhelming to let him Baby her more than occasionally. It was almost scary how deeply she'd fallen into her perfect fantasy the moment he'd put that diaper on her.

She pulled her knees up tighter, trying to get into a little ball, hampered by the bulky material between her legs. The very object that reminded her she was still in a very young headspace.

At least the sexual desire was slightly abated after two intense orgasms. However, as she suckled the pacifier and squeezed the teddy bear against her chest, the crinkle of the diaper reaching her ears, she still felt the edge of arousal. His hand gliding over her tummy reminded her of the pleasure he'd lavished on her body.

"Stop thinking, Baby girl. We'll figure everything out together. You don't have to worry about anything. That's why I'm here. I promise, we'll talk after you nap." He pressed a kiss against her neck and hugged her tight against his body. "Rest now."

Those words enabled Daisy to stop her mind from racing. She relaxed enough to fall into a deep, sated sleep.

Chapter Ten

"Sweet Baby girl, I'm afraid you need to wake up now," her Daddy's voice rumbled in her ear.

Daisy shook her head and squeezed her eyes closed. "I don't wanna."

"I know. I'd rather keep you here as well."

The sad tone of his voice woke her up quickly. Daisy blinked her eyelids to look up at him standing next to the bed. "We have to go back to the real world?"

"I prefer to think of it as the outside world." Bear sat down on the edge of the bed and scooped her up to sit on his lap. "We each have responsibilities and jobs we enjoy. You can't eat nearly as many cupcakes as I can make in a day. And, I only have one nose to sniff, so I can't enjoy all the fragrant floral arrangements you enjoy making."

"I'd hate to close my shop. Flowers always make people happy. I like to celebrate with my clients and help console them during their rough days," Daisy agreed.

She dropped her eyes to stare at his now T-shirt-covered chest. Gathering her courage, Daisy whispered, "Did you like me being Little?"

"You were very brave, Baby girl. I treasure your Little side.

Thank you for daring to reveal your needs and desires to me. I've searched to find my perfect Little for so long—one who would allow me to take care of her completely."

"It wasn't too much?" she asked, peeking up to assess his reaction.

"You couldn't be too Little for me, Baby girl. I promise to be honest with you if you'll return the favor."

Studying his eyes, Daisy could only read positivity and... caring? She smiled at him. "I always try to be honest. But sometimes, I get scared."

"What helps to reassure you when you're frightened?"

"I like to be with someone I trust who cares," she confided.

"I'd like to be that someone," he answered, pulling her close to his body in a gigantic bear hug.

Daisy laid her head on his shoulder and breathed in her Daddy's unique scent. Warmth surrounded her as she rested against his hard frame. The relaxed strength of his body was hard against her, but supportive. She knew he could be both tender and fierce. Circling his neck with her arms, Daisy clung to him.

They sat wrapped together for several seconds before Bear scooped her up into his arms and carried her into the bathroom. He gently undressed her, pressing kisses against her bare skin until she stood naked in front of him. Daisy's usual self-consciousness at being so exposed in front of a man was eased by her Daddy's obvious enjoyment of her form.

With tented pants attesting to his desire, Bear sent her into the shower. "Go, Baby girl. Get clean so you can go play with your flowers."

"You're not coming in with me?" she questioned.

"You'll never make it to work on time if I join you."

His blunt assessment of his desire to make love to her once again sent a wave of heat through her cheeks, and Daisy knew she was blushing furiously. She smiled, however, as she scurried into the stream of water.

"I like knowing that he wants me," she whispered aloud, believing the sound of the water would cover her words from the man who waited outside the stall with a towel.

"Ditto," he called with a laugh.

"Daddy!" Daisy protested. "You weren't supposed to be able to hear me."

"Daddies are always listening to their Littles," he explained. "That's what Daddies do. How else do you think they know everything?"

"Daddy school?" she asked, stepping out of the shower after her quick wash to remove the remains of their lovemaking.

He wrapped the towel around her to soak up the droplets before rubbing her skin to whisk away any wet spots. Bear chuckled as she wiggled eagerly in response to the towel as it pressed between her thighs and buttocks. Her Daddy was very thorough.

"I wish there was a Daddy school. Littles and their Daddies or Mommies usually just figure out things together."

"Like my pacifier earlier?" She felt her face flame back into warmth once again.

"I filled my home with different things I felt a Little girl might need. Pacifiers keep Littles from fretting too much. You needed one this morning. I have bottom pacifiers, too. Sometimes, those are a good distraction as well," Bear explained as he wrapped the towel around her and led Daisy back to her nursery.

"I won't need one of those," she rushed to assure him.

"Your bottom will need attention frequently," her Daddy corrected Daisy. "Temperature time and then into your clothes to head to work."

He led her to the rocking chair and sat down, tugging her forward by the hand he held firmly in his immense grasp. Unfastening the tucked towel, Bear allowed it to drop to the ground, leaving her naked in front of him.

Her nipples clenched into almost painful buds as his eyes

wandered over her body. Daisy closed her eyes as she waited for him to brush an electronic instrument over her forehead. She looked up in surprise as he shifted her body to lie over his hard thighs. To her horror, Daisy saw a large jar of lubricant with a thick thermometer sticking out of the open container.

"No. Don't take my temperature in my bottom," she protested as he held her firmly pinned in place with one forearm against her back as he reached with the other hand to snag the wide glass tube.

Thick, clear lubricant clung to the device. Daisy knew nothing she did could keep it from sliding deep inside her. She clenched her bottom anyway.

"Don't be naughty," her Daddy corrected before spanking her sharply with three punishing swats.

Daisy arched her back in an automatic response to the short-lived pain, unknowingly presenting that small hidden entrance. She tried to tense her bottom to stop the cold, silver tip from sliding into her puckered opening.

"No!" she wailed as it slid deep inside her body. Daisy froze at the feel of the cold glass filling her.

"Hush, Baby girl. You'll get used to me taking care of you. Count to one hundred and it will be time to take it out."

"One, two, three, four, five, six, seven..." She ticked over the numbers as quickly as possible.

"Too fast, Daisy. Say them with me," he directed. "One, Mississippi, two, Mississippi, three..."

"That will take forever!" she protested.

"Each time you argue, we'll start again. One, Mississippi, two, Mississippi."

"Three, Mississippi, four, Mississippi, five..." Daisy bowed to his method of counting. She still said them as fast as she could.

It seemed to take eons before she could announce, "One hundred, Mississippi."

"Good girl," he praised her, sliding the thermometer from her bottom. Bear held her in place as he read the temperature.

"A fraction over normal. I think it registered a bit high because you were upset. Just to be sure, we'll check it again tonight. I want to make sure you're not sick."

"I feel really good," Daisy rushed to assure him.

"I'm glad to hear that." He patted her bare bottom with his free hand.

"Now, a bit of medicine to make sure Daddy didn't hurt you last night when I made love to you. Stand up and go lie down on your changing table on your back," Bear instructed as he cleaned the thermometer with a disposable wipe from the drawer.

Awkwardly, Daisy stood up and walked over to the changing table. A small stool sat next to it, and she clambered up to sit on the edge. Looking back at her Daddy, she saw him press the thermometer back into the lubricant and knew he would use it again. She squeezed her buttocks together, feeling the slickness between them.

Daisy tried to ignore the arousal juices that had gathered between her legs as well. She didn't want to admit that she'd gotten turned on by the treatment. Clenching her thighs together, she silently rebuked herself.

Get it together. Having him put something in your butt shouldn't be stimulating!

"Lie back, Daisy. I have some ointment to apply."

Torn from her thoughts, Daisy shifted to stretch out on the table. Only when he pressed her knees apart to the side did she realize he would see how taking her temperature had affected her.

"I'm okay. I don't need any medicine."

"Daddy makes that decision." Bear pulled a wipe from the container without comment and carefully wiped the evidence of her arousal away. He leaned in to examine her vaginal opening carefully, making her squirm with embarrassment.

"Hold still, Baby girl. There are a few inflamed places here. I'll make it better."

Bear squeezed an inch of blue ointment onto one fingertip. "This is composed of natural herbs as well as a traditional soothing medicine. It will heat a bit as it goes on but will soothe your stretched skin to help it heal."

Before she could process his words, her Daddy spread the medicine around and just inside her opening. Daisy could feel the warmth building as he carefully covered her delicate skin.

"Ooh, it's hot!"

"It will ease up in a few minutes," he assured her as he wiped his fingers on a new cloth before helping her sit up. "Let's get you dressed and on the road to work. I washed your panties last night so they would be clean to wear today and I found clothes in your overnight bag."

Distracted by the warmth between her legs, Daisy needed his assistance to step into her panties and jeans. The heat gathering in her most intimate spaces made her want to rip her clothes off to rub against herself. She knew she would have done this in a flash if she'd been alone. When Daisy pressed her fingers against the seam running between her legs, her Daddy's hand lifted hers away.

"No touching without my permission, Baby girl. The heat will dissipate soon, and you don't want to wipe away the medicine," he corrected her sternly.

"But..."

"No buts." Bear finished dressing her before he took her hand and lead Daisy from the nursery. "Time to go to work. I made you another smoothie. Can you hold it?" He handed her an insulated container from the fridge equipped with a straw.

She allowed him to guide her with an arm around her waist to her car parked in his driveway. Daisy relaxed slightly when she noted there was no evidence of flowers under her windshield wiper. Her Daddy's home was safe.

"Text me when you get to work and let me know you're there safely," he instructed.

"Okay, Daddy."

Sliding behind the wheel, she sighed in relief. The medicine's heat was lessening just as he'd promised. Daisy took a sip of the smoothie before placing it in her cup holder.

"I'll see you soon, Daisy," Bear called as she backed out of his driveway.

Daisy waved furiously and blew several kisses before putting the car into reverse. The route to the floral shop passed quickly as her thoughts darted through her mind. The morning traffic kept her from reliving all their time together in detail. Before she knew it, Daisy was in her normal parking spot behind the store.

"Let's go make some people happy," she told herself aloud with a smile.

Chapter Eleven

The next week flew past in a flurry of petals, cupcakes, and kisses. Daisy spent as much time together with her Daddy as possible. Whether it was in the beautiful nursery he had created or during stolen minutes from their work schedules, she loved being with Bear. He was the best Daddy ever.

Daisy pushed the door open to Little Cakes and waved as the staff members all greeted her by name. "Hi, everyone. Do you think Tarson can take time off for lunch?"

"He better," Ellie answered with a smile. "He's been talking about the picnic lunch he packed for the two of you all morning. We're about ready to break into the basket he brought."

"Bear's a great cook," Daisy commented before laughing. "I'm sure you could have eaten half of what he made. There's always so much food when he makes a meal."

"I'll go tell him you're here," Riley offered and headed through the swinging door into the rear of the cupcake bakery.

"He's been hard at work on a new recipe for Lemon Chiffon cupcakes," Ellie confided. "You'll have to let me know what you think. Supposedly, our original recipe wasn't good enough for his 'Baby girl's favorite cupcake.'" Ellie crooked her fingers in air quotes to show she repeated his words.

"Really?" Daisy smiled broadly. She loved how much her Daddy liked to spoil her.

"Looking at the ingredients he's incorporated into this cupcake, I wish he had girlfriends who loved all the flavors. I'd be a billionaire in just a few weeks," Ellie laughed.

When Daisy's happy expression faltered, Ellie rushed to add, "Bear wouldn't think of having any other girlfriends or Littles other than you. That man is totally smitten."

"That's right. No others for either one of us," Bear confirmed as he came through the door to catch the last of their conversation.

"Hold these for me, Baby girl." He handed Daisy a two-cupcake cardboard container before pressing a quick kiss to her lips.

"You made a special cupcake for me?" she asked, staring up at him.

"My Baby girl's favorite has to be as extraordinary as she is," he answered before gesturing toward the door with a wicker picnic basket.

Bear held out his hand for hers and squeezed her fingers tightly before leading Daisy outside. He chose a bench a few shops down from Little Cakes. "This okay for lunch, sweetheart?"

"It's great! You didn't need to go to so much trouble to make me a special cupcake."

"No trouble. Ellie and I are looking at all the recipes to see if they can be improved. I chose to start with your favorite. We've almost sold out today. Everyone who has tried them bought a few more to take home."

"I'll try mine now," she offered eagerly as she pulled open the small container.

"No, Baby girl. Lunch first, then dessert."

"But..."

"No buts. Close that back up. It will wait. I promise."

Bear opened the basket and pulled out a small container. "Try this. It's a salad with edamame and veggies."

"It looks awfully healthy," Daisy commented, flicking one green bean with a finger.

"It's both good for you and delicious. Try it." Bear handed her a fork and gestured toward the bowl. He pulled out another sealed portion and opened it up.

Daisy watched him take a large bite and chew with enjoyment before she scooped up a small taste. Slowly, she placed the sample in her mouth to try. Crisp freshness tantalized her tastebuds as she ate.

"Yum! This is really good, Daddy," she enthused.

"I'm glad you like it," he answered with a knowing smile.

"Maybe you should open a restaurant?"

"No way. I'd be there day and night and wouldn't have any time to spend with my Little girl. Ellie's business is booming. She decided this morning that she needs me full time."

"Congratulations! This means you won't have to look for another job, right?"

"That's right. I'll work at Little Cakes during the day and at Blaze in the evenings that you wish to go visit the club. Evan is ready to take over for me if I'm not there."

"That's perfect," she celebrated before taking another bite of salad.

"Everything seems to be falling into place. What do you think about painting flowers in the nursery one day soon?" he asked, naming a day when both Little Cakes and Blooms by Daisy were closed.

"I'd love that." She hesitated for a minute before adding, "Unless you'd rather not. The room is beautiful as it is."

"No way. I think you're right. It needs flowers everywhere to match the Little girl I created it for."

"I won't go crazy," she promised.

"Maybe I will," he suggested, taking the empty container from her.

"Is it all gone? That was yummy."

"I'll make more for you. Here, try this next." He offered her half a sandwich.

Daisy took a bite and chewed. It was good. She just liked the salad better. Eyeing his still full container, she suggested, "You wouldn't want to swap, would you?"

Laughing, he handed her his bowl. "Eat, Baby girl."

He polished off her surrendered half sandwich in three bites. When he offered her another half, Daisy lifted the bowl toward him to indicate she had more left to eat.

"This was so good," she complimented when the bowl was empty. Daisy ran a finger along the sides to pick up the last few morsels that had escaped her fork.

"I'm glad you liked it. Want part of a sandwich or your cupcake now?"

"Cupcake."

Daisy watched him open the box and extract one perfect yellow cupcake. Shocked at the sight of it out of the box, she dropped her jaw open as the white chocolate daisy decoration appeared pressed into the side of the frosting. "Do all of them have a flower?"

"Yes. And not just a flower, but a daisy."

Tears sprang to her eyes. "You made this for me?"

"Don't cry, Baby girl. You haven't even taken a bite yet," he teased. "That's going to make you weep again."

She peeled back the wrapper and took a small bite, trying to get both frosting and cake. Delicious lemon flavor burst across her tastebuds. Daisy chewed quickly and took a larger taste.

"Good, huh?"

"This is the best," she mumbled.

"Eat, then talk."

Daisy swallowed and held the cupcake up to her nose to sniff. Looking at her Daddy over the frosting, she whispered, "I could live on these," before taking another large bite.

"No, Baby girl. Cupcakes are a delicious treat, but not good for you to eat as every meal. You have to eat something from all the food groups to be healthy."

"This has to have grains, fruit, and dairy in it," she protested.

"Looks like I'm going to be in charge of making sure you eat properly," he observed.

Daisy nodded her agreement with that statement before taking another bite and rolling her eyes upward in ecstasy.

"I can have these still, right?"

"As a special treat, definitely."

"Yay! Are you going to eat yours?" she asked, eyeing his dessert still sitting in the box.

"You wouldn't rob your Daddy of a cupcake, would you?"

"With those cupcakes? Definitely, yes!"

Daisy waited for Bear to answer but he was distracted. She followed his line of sight to focus on a battered sedan that cruised through the shopping area. "Do you know that person?"

"The tinted window keeps me from seeing who it is. The car has passed us three times."

"That's weird. Maybe they're searching for a shop," Daisy suggested.

"Maybe."

"What color of paint should I get for the flowers?" Daisy questioned to distract him. She was pleased when Bear pulled his attention from the taillights of the car exiting the strip center to concentrate on her once again.

"I guess that depends on the type of flowers you want to create."

"Let's just get a bunch of pretty colors and see what happens."

"Good idea, Baby girl. We'll go get a variety after work tonight before we head to Blaze." He pulled out his phone. "I'll create a new note so we'll remember what we need."

Soon, it was time for them to return to work. As they passed

Little Cakes, Daisy poked her head inside to give Ellie a thumbs up.

"Good cupcake, huh?" the bakery owner suggested.

"Good doesn't even come close," Daisy assured her.

Chapter Twelve

Humming a popular song as she tidied the front counter, Daisy kept an eye on the door as it ticked down to closing time. On her schedule for tonight was paint shopping, dinner, and a visit to Blaze. Bear was working tonight and she couldn't wait to hang out with him and her friends.

Daisy was going to try out a few designs for flowers on paper before slathering paint on the wall. She hoped some others would paint with her tonight.

When her door opened, Daisy looked up with a smile that quickly froze on her lips. She forced herself to be professional. It could be a coincidence that he was there.

"So, this is where you hide during the day," Leo Miller commented with a smile that didn't quite make it to his eyes.

"Are you interested in ordering some flowers?" she asked, stiffening her back to resist curling into a ball.

"Flowers do fascinate me. I particularly like daisies—even when they misbehave."

His words felt like oil to her skin. They oozed over her. She tilted her chin up and answered, "Flowers can't misbehave. They respond well to someone who respects their special attributes and creates an arrangement that highlights them positively."

"I see that you haven't learned to respect your Daddy."

"I respect my Daddy. I don't follow the wishes of others who try to step into that role without building a relationship with me," Daisy answered defiantly. She pulled her phone from her pocket and searched for Bear's number in her directory.

"You are extremely naughty, Little girl. It's a good thing I know how to deal with rebellious Littles," he answered, walking forward to brace his palms on the counter.

Her fingers flew over her phone as her heartrate skyrocketed. Fumbling, she selected the wrong number and hung up as her aunt Teresa answered the phone. She'd call her back later.

Daddy! Daisy touched the call emblem as she backed away from the counter to put more room between herself and the man who called himself Daddy Leo.

"Baby girl," Bear's growly voice held delight to hear from her. "I'm almost there to pick you up."

"Daddy! He's here."

"Who's there, Baby girl?"

"Daddy Leo."

"Lock the door."

"No! He's inside."

"Put me on speaker."

Daisy's trembling finger quickly pressed the audio button to switch him to speaker.

"Got it," she whispered.

"Leo, this is Tarson Kirkwood. I am two blocks away. Get out of there now or just being banned from Blaze will be the least of your worries."

"Tarson, I'm sure Daisy will be glad to play with both of us. There's no need for this aggressive reaction," Leo answered smoothly as he pushed away from the counter. With a wink at Daisy, the unwanted visitor walked to the door and disappeared.

"Listen, asshole..." Bear began.

Daisy couldn't hear the rest of what he said because she dropped the phone onto the wooden surface to run around the partition to flip the deadbolt closed.

"Daisy!" he shouted as she returned to the counter to pick up the cell.

"I'm okay. He just left. I locked the door."

"One block away. Damn this traffic. I'm almost there. Stay inside," he demanded.

Five minutes later, Daisy heard the squeal of tires before heavy steps ran to her front entrance. Huddled out of sight from anyone looking through the glass at the entrance, she waited until she heard his voice.

"Daisy? It's me, Baby girl. Let me in."

Flying to the door, she fumbled with the lock before throwing the barrier open and flinging herself into his arms. She buried her face against his broad chest. "I was so scared. Is he still out there?"

"The parking spaces in front are all empty now. He scurried away like cockroaches usually do," Bear growled.

"Thank you for coming to save me," she whispered as she looked up at his face.

The concern etched into his features made her rise onto her toes to press her lips against his. The fiery kiss that followed made Daisy feel as if he'd marked his possession on her heart. She slid her hands up his torso to wrap around his neck. Clinging to his strong body, Daisy put all her emotions into the next kiss as she claimed him as hers as well.

Bear's mouth gentled on hers. Seemingly reassured that she was unharmed and he had reached her in time, he seduced her with long, slow kisses that ramped up their breathing for an entirely different reason than the adrenaline rush that Leo's visit had evoked. When her hands drifted back down his chiseled chest to slide under Bear's snug T-shirt, he set her a few inches away from his body as he pressed her fingers against his abdomen.

"We need to call Wyatt."

"Later?" she suggested, trying to wiggle her fingers away from his control to trace the hardness pressing against his fly.

"Now."

Stepping back a bit farther before snagging his phone from his back pocket, Bear called the detective and reported the incident. Eventually, he put the phone on speaker so Daisy could answer the police officer's questions.

"Okay. I've made some notes to update the file. Unfortunately, since he came through an unlocked door into the shop during regular business hours and didn't touch Daisy, there's not a lot I can do. I've got his address and will drive over there tonight to warn Leo he needs to keep his distance. Without a restraining order, that's the most I can do," Wyatt informed them.

"We have to wait until he hurts her? That's screwed up!" Bear scowled.

"It is. Daisy, stay vigilant and call if you need help. Even if you're just spooked by something you can't really explain, call," the detective urged.

Daisy nodded before realizing he couldn't see her through the phone. "I will. Promise."

"Good girl. I'll be in touch." The detective disconnected.

"Come on, Baby girl. It's time to get out of here. Ready to go get some pretty paint?"

She knew he was trying to distract her. Daisy nodded, putting on a brave face. "I'd like that."

After turning off all the lights, she slipped her hand into Bear's and allowed him to guide her out the front door of Blooms by Daisy. She looked back in the side mirror as they drove away. The store had always been a haven for her. Working with flowers and her customers invigorated her. When a shiver of apprehension glided down her spine, Daisy sat straight up in indignation.

"Something wrong?" Bear asked in concern.

"I'm not going to let him make me scared. I'm not going to give him that power," she declared.

"That's my girl." Bear wrapped his fingers around her thigh and squeezed. "Be smart but don't let him steal the joy from your life."

Daisy nodded. Pushing Leo from her mind, she changed the subject and warned, "We're getting bright colors for the flowers."

"How bright is bright?" he asked with a theatrical wince visible even in the dim glow of the overhead streetlights.

Her laughter filled the car, dispelling any lingering negativity. "What do you think of fuchsia?"

"Is that even a color?" he teased.

"Daddy!"

Armed with a cart full of small paint cans, brushes, and drop cloths, they emerged an hour later from the home improvement store. Daisy skipped happily, clinging to the basket with one hand.

"See, you didn't lose me," she pointed out to the large man pushing the cart.

"I've marked down in my Daddy book that my Baby girl is always required to hold on to my hand or the cart. You're a speed demon in those aisles."

"Your Daddy book," she scoffed. "And I can't help it that you're slow."

"Sometimes slow is good, Baby girl," he answered playfully, waggling his eyebrows meaningfully at her.

"I may need you to remind me of that."

"Challenge accepted," he declared as warmth kindled in his gaze. "Let's get this all loaded into the trunk, and I'll take you home to refresh your memory."

They loaded the supplies into the trunk with frequent

breaks for kisses. As they finished, Bear swatted the pert bottom wiggling in front of him as Daisy leaned inside to make sure nothing would fall over on the ride home.

"Hey!" she protested, turning around to glare at him. "I'm being good."

"Sometimes, a reminder is important," he said with a wink.

She turned back toward the trunk and mumbled under her breath, "Maybe Daddies need a spanking."

His answering swat made her squeal.

"Listen to your Daddy," a kindly older voice advised from behind them in the parking lot.

Daisy popped up to turn to look at the woman in her eighties, holding her equally mature companion's hand. "Yes, Ma'am," she answered before looking with disbelief at Bear.

His expression revealed the battle to keep himself from laughing aloud. "Come on, Baby girl. It's time to go home. We have just enough time to unload the paint and grab a bite to eat before we head to Blaze." He swept her into the front seat as the older couple unloaded their cart.

Looking out her window, Daisy watched the man lean in to fasten his companion's seatbelt. "Were they really...?" Her voice drifted away as she considered her future with Bear.

"Daddies always keep their Little girls close," he responded, squeezing her hand as they headed home.

Chapter Thirteen

"Thanks for inviting me to visit Blaze tonight. It's been a long week. I could really use some downtime." Wyatt adjusted the front of his black shirt as he joined Tarson in the main room of Blaze.

"You're welcome. I'm glad you could come. Sorry it was such short notice. When we spoke to you earlier this evening, I remembered you'd shown an interest."

"I appreciate the text." Wyatt looked around. "Impressive place."

"One of the best," Tarson agreed proudly. "I've been one of the dungeon masters here for a while now." He grinned. "I'm about to cut way back on the number of nights I work here, though."

Wyatt smiled. "I can see why. You're a lucky man." He slapped Tarson on the shoulder. "Daisy seems like the sweetest Little girl. I hate that she's had not one, but two scares in her store. I'm keeping a closer eye on that strip mall, as are the rest of the officers I work with."

Tarson glanced at Wyatt. "Thank you. I appreciate it."

Wyatt looked around. "Where is she? Did she come with you tonight?"

Tarson nodded. "Yep. She's in the daycare. It's a separate area inside the club where Littles can hang out with other Littles in a safe environment."

Wyatt grinned. "I love that."

Tarson nodded over his shoulder. "Come on. I'll show you the daycare area." Tarson certainly didn't mind playing tour guide for the potential new member. Plus, he would get to check on Daisy without hovering.

Daisy was having a painting party tonight. She'd gathered a few other Littles to help her sketch and paint flowers which she intended to use as samples when they painted the actual room in his house.

Sure enough, Tarson couldn't keep the grin off his face as he spotted Daisy with three of her friends—Riley, Lark, and Ellie.

"They look like they're having fun," Wyatt commented.

Tarson nodded. He knew he had a goofy grin on his face, but he didn't care. He was head over heels for his Baby girl. Watching her leaning over a large piece of paper, carefully painting inside the lines of a flower he was certain she'd sketched, made his heart happy. She even had her tongue sticking out to one side in concentration.

"Hey, I recognize all those other women from Little Cakes. I met them a few times while dealing with those young thugs." He took a step closer. "Uh, isn't that Lark Adams?"

"Yes. She's Ellie's best friend."

"I didn't know she was Little." Wyatt took a few steps closer, his brows raised as he glanced at Tarson.

"I don't know. She's a guest like you. She's never been here before. Ellie conned her into helping with the flower painting."

"Hmmm." Wyatt shifted his gaze back to the girls.

Tarson wondered if Wyatt had a thing for Lark. He sure seemed interested. If it were possible to actually see light bulbs lighting up over a person's head, Tarson was pretty sure he would be seeing them now over Wyatt.

"Did you know Officer Wyatt was at Blaze earlier tonight, Daddy?" Daisy asked as soon as Tarson started the engine and put his car in drive.

"Yep. I invited him to come on a visitor's pass." Tarson set his hand on Daisy's bare thigh as he pulled out of the parking lot.

Daisy giggled. "I think he has a thing for Lark."

Tarson chuckled. "You do, do you? What makes you say that?" He was curious to find out how his Baby girl came to that conclusion. Tarson had left Wyatt to his own defenses after giving him a tour. After all, Tarson had been there to work tonight.

"Well, for one thing, Ellie said so. She was teasing Lark. Riley agreed. They said they thought Wyatt showed particular interest in Lark when he came into Little Cakes after those thugs were apprehended."

Tarson gave her thigh a squeeze. "Don't let your imagination get carried away, Baby girl," he warned. "You're speculating. Besides, just because Lark agreed to paint with you tonight doesn't mean she's Little."

Daisy sighed, her shoulders dropping. "True. And we know Wyatt is a Daddy because he told us so."

When Tarson came to a stop light, he turned to face Daisy and gave her a stern look. "No matchmaking. You let the two of them figure things out for themselves, understood?"

Daisy reached up and twirled a lock of her blonde hair, not meeting his gaze.

"Daisy..." he warned.

She hmphed. "Daddy, you're no fun. Ellie and Riley and I were going to come up with ways to make sure the two of them run into each other."

"Baby girl, wipe that idea from your mind. I'm certain if Garrett knew his Little was playing matchmaker, he would spank her bottom. And when we get home, that's what I'm going to do to you to make sure I've made my point." He lifted a brow.

Daisy pushed out her bottom lip and pouted, crossing her arms dramatically. "I didn't do anything wrong," she muttered.

"You thought about it though. I can see the wheels turning in your head, Baby girl." He started driving again when the light turned green.

Other than a few swats now and then, Tarson had yet to give Daisy a full spanking. Tonight was a good night to make sure she knew that Daddy was serious. No meddling.

Daisy was silent most of the rest of the way home, and she remained that way as he helped her out of the car and led her into the house.

It was late, but he knew she hadn't eaten anything for several hours, so he paused in the kitchen. "How about some milk before bed?"

She glanced at him sideways. "Are you still going to spank me?"

"Yes. But afterward, you might like a bottle of milk while I rock you and snuggle with you. I even have strawberry or chocolate flavoring if you'd like."

Her shoulders dropped. She was almost too cute to keep a straight face. "Fine. I'll have strawberry."

He lifted her chin and met her gaze. "Would you like to ask in a nicer tone, Baby girl?"

"Sorry, Daddy. May I please have strawberry milk after you spank my bottom?"

Her sassy voice made it even more difficult for him to not break form and start laughing. "Daisy, judging by your attitude, I'm starting to think you're practically begging me to spank you."

She lowered her gaze but said nothing.

Tarson had been mostly joking, but now he wondered. He watched her shuffling her shoe across the floor in front of her

LEMON CHIFFON

while he made her milk. She certainly hadn't denied his off-the-cuff accusation.

Without a word, he led her to the nursery, set the bottle of milk on the floor, and lowered onto the rocking chair. "Come here, Baby girl," he said gently, reaching for her to close the distance between them.

She took her sweet time getting to him, which added to his amusement. Where was this naughty side coming from?

When she was close enough, he held her hips and angled her between his thighs. "What's going through that mind of yours, Baby girl?"

She shrugged, her face still lowered. He could just catch the glimpse of pink in her cheeks. Maybe she really *did* want him to spank her. He should have thought of that. After the way she eagerly accepted trying a pacifier, wearing a diaper, and taking a bottle, it would stand to reason she might fantasize about being spanked, too.

"Has anyone ever spanked you, Daisy?"

She took a slow deep breath. "Not really, Daddy. That bad Daddy Leo only managed a few swats, but they were hard. And you spanked me when I fought against the, uh... Well, earlier."

He lifted her chin, forcing her to meet his gaze. Her cheeks were indeed red now. "Don't think I've forgotten about the thermometer, Baby girl. Just because you didn't mention it doesn't mean I don't remember."

She sighed and shuffled her feet. "I don't need my temperature taken again, Daddy. I feel fine."

"Who decides how to best take care of his Baby girl?"

Another dramatic sigh. "You do, Daddy," she whispered.

"That's right, and that includes disciplining you when you misbehave, doesn't it?"

"Yes, Sir," she murmured.

"I have a question, and I want you to answer me honestly, Daisy." He drew his brows together as he made sure she was looking at him.

She licked her lips.

"Is being spanked one of the things you've fantasized about but never really experienced?"

She hesitated a few seconds before slowly nodding.

He released her chin and pulled her into his arms, holding her tight. After smoothing his hand down her braids, he tipped her head back again. "There's nothing to be embarrassed about, Baby girl. Lots of Littles like to have their bottoms spanked."

"I don't really know if I do or not, Daddy. I just want to try it."

"And you will. Right now. And then we'll talk about how it made you feel. Okay?"

"Yes, Sir."

"Good girl." He lifted her up onto his knee and leaned over to remove her shoes and socks before setting her back on her feet and unzipping her dress down her back.

Tonight's dress was white with yellow daisies all over it. It was a wonder she'd managed to paint without getting anything on it, though he had noticed she'd worn a smock while she'd been painting.

As he lowered the dress to the floor, she set her hands on his shoulders so she could step out of the material. She was left in nothing but her panties. He knew she sometimes wore an athletic bra on nights when she went to the club, but he hadn't given her any bra when he'd dressed her earlier, and she hadn't seemed to mind.

When he reached for the elastic of her panties, she flinched. "Can I keep my panties, Daddy?"

"No, Baby girl. Daddy is going to spank your bare bottom this time. It heightens the experience, but in addition, it lets me see how pink your skin is getting so I'll know how hard to swat you."

She shuddered. "I don't think you'll need to spank me very hard, Daddy."

He chuckled. "Is that so, Baby girl? Who do you think will decide that?"

She blew out a defeated breath. "You, Daddy."

"Exactly." He angled her to one side and leaned her over his lap. Her feet didn't reach the floor, so she wouldn't be able to get any traction. In addition, he lifted both her arms and drew them to the small of her back. For this first spanking, he wanted to be sure she didn't try to reach back with her hands. He wouldn't risk accidentally swatting her fingers.

She whimpered when he set his palm on her pretty bottom. Twisting her head so she could look at him, she asked, "What if I don't like it, Daddy?"

"You're not supposed to like it, Baby girl. Spanking wouldn't be a good deterrent if you enjoyed it, but don't you worry, Daddy will make sure to spank you just the right amount. Not so hard that you hate being spanked, but hard enough that you think twice about being naughty in the future."

"Yes, Sir." She leaned her cheek on his thigh and seemed resigned.

Tarson knew how important this was. Far more important than when he diapered her or fed her a bottle. He needed to watch her closely to make sure he was meeting her needs without going too far.

Some Little girls loved being spanked. Some loved it so much they intentionally misbehaved to earn a good spanking.

Tarson doubted Daisy would ever intentionally act up. It wasn't in her nature. The only reason she'd done so tonight was because she was curious and anxious for this experience.

He intended to give his Baby girl exactly what she craved.

Chapter Fourteen

Daisy clenched her butt cheeks together in anticipation of the first swat. She had very little experience to draw on.

Daddy was right, however; she was curious. She'd definitely fantasized about what it would be like to have a Daddy swat her bottom. It certainly wasn't something she could do herself.

If she'd been determined, she could have fixed bottles, worn diapers, or sucked a pacifier when she was pretending alone, but spanking had never been a possibility.

"Daddy is going to start out softly and build up, Baby girl."

She held her breath. She knew he wouldn't hurt her. He'd never intentionally cause her harm. But she was still nervous.

When he lifted his hand and delivered the first swat to her right cheek, she flinched. It wasn't bad though. Not bad at all.

The next spank landed on her left cheek. She flinched less than the first time. Maybe this wasn't so bad. In fact, maybe it was nothing to worry about at all.

Daddy swatted her several more times, switching it up so she never knew where the next slap might land. It was starting to sting, and she squirmed as her skin heated.

He rubbed her bottom after about a half dozen spanks. "How're you doing, Daisy?"

"Okay, Daddy."

"Can you take more?"

"Yes, Sir," she whispered, somewhat embarrassed. It would be easier if he didn't make her interact with him while he delivered her punishment, but that wouldn't make him a very good Daddy, she reasoned.

A dozen more slaps rained down on her, covering her bottom and the backs of her thighs. When Daddy paused to rub her heated skin again, he commented, "You're doing so well, Baby girl. Daddy is proud of you. And your bottom is so pretty, all pink with my handprints. May I keep going?"

She nodded.

"Words, Baby girl."

"Yes, Daddy. Please keep going."

"Good girl."

She lost count of how many times he spanked her. In fact, she relaxed against his lap. It was rather cathartic. Instead of feeling tense and angry, she felt the stress ebbing from her body.

Suddenly, he swatted her in a new spot, right at the base of her bottom where her cheeks met her thighs. The vibrations went to her pussy and she arched her chest in surprise.

Daddy stopped and rubbed the spot, leaving her with a new sensation. She was quivering with arousal. "Daddy?" She squirmed on his lap.

"I think my Baby girl enjoyed that last part a bit too much."

She sighed. He knew. Mortified by her body's response, she turned her face toward the floor, not wanting him to see how pink her cheeks were.

Daddy smoothed his hand all over her bottom for several more seconds before rolling her over and cradling her in his arms. He gave the rocking chair a push as he cuddled her against him.

He kissed her temple. "I'm so proud of you, Baby girl."

She was trembling with need.

He stroked her back, keeping her sore bottom between his

thighs. "No reason to be embarrassed, Daisy. You aren't the first Baby girl to enjoy a spanking."

She finally tipped her head back to look at him. "Really?"

"Of course. Why do you think so many Littles misbehave on a regular basis?"

She shrugged. "I thought they liked the pain."

"Some of them do. For lots of Littles, the pain is the goal. It helps them relieve stress. That was true for you, too, until I hit the sweet spot."

She swallowed. "Now my pussy is throbbing, Daddy."

He smiled. "I know it is. Would you like Daddy to make it feel better?"

She nodded immediately, relieved he was offering. "Please, Daddy."

He narrowed his gaze at her. "I won't always let you come after a punishment spanking, Baby girl, so don't get any ideas. Tonight, I'm going to because you've been so brave."

She nodded again. "Okay, Daddy."

He stood and carried her to the changing table before depositing her on top.

She was surprised, and even more so when he strapped her down, including her knees in a wide-open position. By the time he was finished restraining her, she was squirming with need. Her bottom hurt every time she rubbed it against the changing table padding, but that only added to her arousal.

Daddy cupped her face with one hand, stroking her cheek.

She leaned into his touch. It took every ounce of her strength not to beg him to touch her pussy.

His other hand finally landed on her inner thigh, but he never took his gaze from hers. He stroked her sensitive skin, coming closer and closer to her pussy.

She grew wetter and hotter and needier with every passing moment until she was eventually panting and trying to arch her butt off the table. She was far too secured to wiggle around much though.

"My Baby girl is so needy, isn't she?" Daddy asked.

"Please, Daddy," she finally begged.

He slid his fingers lower, parting her labia without looking. She wondered if he had eyes in the side of his head the way he so expertly touched her without touching her any place important.

The exposure from her parted labia intensified her desire tenfold. Her clit was throbbing. Her nipples were hard points and he hadn't even touched them.

A low deep moan escaped her lips the moment he eased a finger deep into her pussy. His motions were controlled and slow. His palm pressed against her clit as he reached as deeply as possible.

Daisy thought she might fall apart if he didn't let her come soon. She'd never been this desperate, not even when they'd had sex. She was experiencing a whole new side of submission.

Daddy eased his finger out of her tight channel, making her whimper from the loss. He held her gaze as he moved that soaked finger lower and circled her tighter hole.

She clenched her bottom. "Daddy..." She wasn't at all sure she wanted him to touch her there. He'd done so earlier with the thermometer, but that was much smaller than his finger.

"Relax your bottom for me, Baby girl. No part of you is off limits to Daddy. Let Daddy slide his finger into your rectum. I promise you'll find out it feels amazing."

She pursed her lips. She didn't believe him. Surely it wouldn't feel good? It would only be embarrassing.

He circled the puckered skin again and tapped it several times before easing the tip of his finger into her forbidden hole. He took his time, entering her a tiny bit at a time.

She held her breath as he gradually deepened the penetration. It didn't hurt, but it felt strange.

Suddenly, his thumb landed on her clit, and she cried out unexpectedly.

"That's my good girl. Let it feel good." He pushed his finger the rest of the way into her bottom while rubbing her clit at the same time.

His thumb stroked her cheek. "Such a good girl letting Daddy penetrate your bottom." He thrust his thumb into her pussy, dragging more of her wetness to her clit and rubbing it so fast that she lost all control.

Daisy tipped her head back, her mouth falling open as her orgasm consumed her. Her pussy clenched at nothing. Her clit throbbed. But her tight rear hole pulsed with her release.

He was right. It felt so good. It was different, but not in a bad way. And as her release ebbed away, she couldn't help but smile. "Thank you, Daddy."

He leaned over and kissed her lips gently. "You're welcome, Baby girl. Thank you for trusting Daddy to know what you need."

She was still trembling from the aftereffects of her orgasm as he cleaned his fingers on a wipe and then reached for the thermometer.

This time she didn't complain as the cold glass slid into her bottom. She was still embarrassed and didn't think she needed her temperature taken, but she didn't argue with her Daddy. He'd proven that he did indeed know best and she needed to trust him.

Without a word, she breathed heavily while she waited for Daddy to remove the thermometer. "No fever. It must have been a fluke earlier." He cleaned off the glass rod, put it back in the jar of lube, and slid a diaper under her bottom.

Moments later, he released her restraints, helped her sit, and pulled a pink nightie over her head. Next, he lifted her into his arms and carried her to the rocking chair.

"I bet my Baby girl is tired."

"Yes, Daddy." She snuggled against him, not wanting him to put her to bed just yet. "And thirsty. Can I have my milk now?"

He leaned down to grab the bottle and brought the nipple

to her lips. He was smiling as if he'd won the lottery while she set her hand over his and let him feed her.

She was pretty sure she was the one who'd won the lottery. Daddy was slowly fulfilling all her dreams. Could he be the one? Her permanent Daddy? Someone she could grow old with like the couple they'd seen in the parking lot earlier?

The thought was scary. This was all so new. There were no guarantees this relationship could last forever and ever.

So many thoughts went through her mind while she suckled the nipple and drank the milk. She knew he was serious about her or he wouldn't be letting her paint flowers on the nursery walls, would he?

He'd said she was his Baby girl so many times she'd lost count. He was so in tune with her needs that he seemed to pluck every fantasy she'd ever had right out of her mind.

She closed her eyes as bad thoughts came to the surface. What if someone came into her store and actually hurt her one of these days? It infuriated her that twice now she'd been threatened in her own store. Blooms by Daisy was supposed to be her special place.

"Hey there," Daddy said as she finished the bottle. "Why the furrowed brow?"

"I was just thinking about Daddy Leo and those thugs from before. Why do people keep threatening me?"

He rubbed her back, rocking her gently. She knew he hated that anyone, let alone several people, had upset his Little girl. "I don't know, Baby girl. It makes Daddy very angry. Wyatt said he'll be increasing patrols in the area though. I'm going to get you set up with a panic button behind the counter, too."

"A panic button?"

"Yep. I'll install it under the register. That way if anyone ever makes you uncomfortable, you can simply push it to alert the police. You won't have to fumble around with your phone."

"Oh. That might make me feel safer."

"That's the plan." Daddy kissed her head. "I know it's late, but how about if Daddy gives you a warm bath before tucking you into bed?"

"That sounds nice, Daddy." She squirmed on his lap. They'd checked a lot of things off her mental list of fantasies, but he kept coming up with more of them.

Daisy had always wondered what it would be like to have a Daddy bathe her. She certainly couldn't do that alone.

"It will sooth your bottom a bit and we can wash your fears right down the drain." He rose, holding her in his arms to carry her into the bathroom.

After setting her on her feet, he turned on the water to fill the tub and then removed her nightie and diaper.

It wasn't as difficult to stand in front of him naked anymore. She liked the way he looked at her, and she loved the way he touched her.

He unraveled her braids next and then used one of the hairbands to gather her hair on the top of her head. When he was done, he turned her toward the mirror. "See? Lemon chiffon."

She giggled. He was right. Her hair did look like a pile of frosting. She was still smiling as he settled her in the tub and reached for a loofah.

"Do you have bubbles, Daddy?"

"I do, but we'll save those for another time. This will be a quick bath." He poured floral-smelling soap on the loofah and reached for her hand.

She wished they had more time. It felt so good when he washed her. She loved how the loofah felt gliding over her skin under his control instead of hers. He didn't leave any part of her unwashed. He even set the loofah aside to wash between her legs with his fingers.

She was flushed from the warm water and his touch as he released the water, sad that the bath was already over. She couldn't wait for a day when they would have more time so she could enjoy his care longer.

"See?" Daddy pointed at the drain as the water swirled away.

"See what, Daddy?"

"We washed your fears down the drain. Don't you see them?"

She giggled. "Oh, I do see them."

"Now my Baby girl can sleep like a rock." He lifted her out of the tub and set her on her feet to dry her.

"Can I sleep with you in your bed, Daddy?" She bit her lip, uncertain what his response would be.

"I think that's a great idea. That way I can hold you in my arms and if you have bad dreams, I can chase them away."

She smiled as he lifted her off her feet and carried her into his bedroom to set her on the big bed. He grabbed a diaper from a drawer in his nightstand and slid it under her before fastening it.

She squirmed as he patted between her legs. "My Baby girl enjoys being younger sometimes, doesn't she?"

"Yes, Daddy," she whispered. It was still hard to admit that. She hoped he didn't mind. She wasn't positive how he felt about the amount of time she spent in such a young headspace in his house.

"Don't move." He palmed her naked tummy and then left the room. A moment later he was back with her nightie, the stuffed bear, and a pacifier. He'd thought of everything.

"Does this poor bear have a name yet?" Daddy asked after he slid the T-shirt over her head. "He's going to get tired of being called just *bear* soon."

Her eyes shot wide. "Do *you* get tired of being called *bear*, Daddy?"

He chuckled. "No. I suppose not." He tickled her tummy. "Though Teddy is a bit silly."

She giggled as she shoved his hand away. "I think I'll call him *Bear* then." She held him up for Daddy to look. "See? He's smiling. He likes the name."

"I suppose you're right." Daddy slid her to the center of the bed and pulled the covers over her. "I'll be right back. Just going to make sure the doors are locked and turn the lights out."

"Are you afraid I might fall off the bed? Is that why you put me in the center, Daddy?"

He dropped his hands down next to her and kissed her lips. "Nope. But when I climb into bed next to you, I'm going to want to drag you into my arms. I won't want you sleeping so far away that you're in another zip code."

She giggled. Her cheeks heated as she watched him leave the room.

He was the best Daddy in the world, and he really did wash her fears down the drain. Now she just needed to convince herself he was really all hers forever and ever.

Chapter Fifteen

Mondays were the best day of the week. It was the only day Blooms by Daisy was closed. This Monday was going to be particularly fun because Daisy was all set to paint flowers around the nursery this afternoon.

She had help, too. Ellie would be there any minute to paint with her. Daddy wanted her to have a friend over. Plus, he and Garrett were going to go install the panic button in her shop. They were putting one in Little Cakes, too.

Daddy had moved all the furniture to the center of the room and covered it with tarps. He'd also laid plastic down on the floor and taped it to the baseboards so no paint would get on the carpet.

Daisy was giddy with excitement when she heard the doorbell and darted toward the front of the house.

"Slow down, Baby girl," Daddy admonished as he followed her. "Let Daddy make sure who it is before you open the door, Daisy."

"Yes, Sir." She came to a stop, but she could see her friend through the window, so she was bouncing on her toes as Daddy let them in.

While Ellie hugged Daisy, Daddy shook Garrett's hand. "Thanks for bringing Ellie over to keep Daisy company."

"Thank *you* for coming up with the panic button idea. I'm going to feel much better after we have those installed," Garrett said.

"Daddy, would you mind stopping by my condo to grab me some clean clothes? I bet there's a pile of mail on the floor, too. The mailman pushes it through a slot on the door." Daisy hadn't been home in a few days. If she ended up painting until late in the evening and staying here another night, she would need clothes for work tomorrow.

"I sure will, Baby girl." He kissed the top of her head. "You two be good. I left you a tray of little sandwiches in the fridge if you get hungry before we get back."

"Thank you, Daddy." Daisy rose onto her toes and pulled his head down for a kiss.

"Lock this door behind us," he commanded as he and Garrett left the house.

As soon as the door clicked closed behind them, the two Littles looked at each other and grinned.

"I'm sorry Riley and Lark couldn't come today, but I'm glad you're here. We're going to have so much fun. Ready to make my nursery beautiful?" Daisy questioned.

"I'm not an amazing artist," Ellie began.

"I've seen your decorating skills. Just pretend you're making icing flowers," Daisy suggested.

"I can do that!"

The two gathered all the colors Daisy and her Daddy had selected, popping lids off the cans and arming themselves with brushes.

"Pick a color and a spot. We'll add the stems later," Daisy suggested.

Working side by side so they could chatter, the two Littles made their first strokes on the wall. Soon, gorgeous flowers decorated the walls. Daisies appeared on each wall of course, but roses, violets, pansies, and many more colorful blooms joined them. Finally, Daisy stepped back from the wall with her paintbrush tinged with green after adding one final leaf.

Dropping to the floor, the Littles looked around in wonder.

"I want us to paint my nursery next," Ellie suggested.

"I owe you a favor. Just let me know when you're ready. What do you want on your walls?" Daisy asked without looking away from the garden in front of them.

"My Daddy suggested a rainbow, but I think cupcakes."

"That would be so cute. What flavors would you include?" Daisy turned her head to meet Ellie's gaze.

"Rainbow Sprinkles, Red Velvet, Key Lime..."

"Lemon Chiffon?" Daisy suggested.

"Is that your favorite?" Ellie guessed.

"Yes. I love yellow and lemon—Yum!"

"Then you'll have to paint a gorgeous Lemon Chiffon cupcake for me!"

"I'd love that!"

"You'll have to remember to put a green dot on the wrapper," Ellie declared.

"Really? Why?"

Ellie reached the paintbrush out and put a dot on Daisy's arm.

Daisy giggled at the feel of the brush moving over her skin. Armed with her own paintbrush, she decorated Ellie's hand with a green squiggle.

Both Littles admired the decoration on their skin. Simultaneously, they turned to consider the cans of paint.

"We'll get in so much trouble if we get paint everywhere," Ellie pointed out.

"Daddy Little-proofed this room. I don't think we can make too much of a mess in here," Daisy reassured her. "Let's reopen the flower colors. I want to practice making a lemon chiffon cupcake."

"Can you put it on my arm? Like a tattoo?" Ellie asked, running over to grab another paintbrush.

She held it out to Daisy. "Here!"

Twenty minutes later, the two Littles froze as they heard the door rattle.

"Daisy! We're home!"

"Uh, oh," Ellie whispered.

"What do we have here?" Garrett asked in wonder as he stepped into the room.

Ellie and Daisy had painted each other with all sorts of cupcakes to practice for the cupcake baker's room. The two Littles grinned at the two men. They were having the best time.

"You ran out of walls, so you decorated yourselves?" Bear asked with a grin that reassured them they weren't in big trouble.

"Ellie wants cupcakes on her nursery walls. We finished with all the flowers, so we thought we'd try a few out," Daisy explained.

"This room is gorgeous. I love the flowers," Garrett complimented. "I think these two Picassos should add some cupcakes to Ellie's room."

Bear turned in a circle, carefully examining all the decorations. "I like this a lot. It's like a garden. Perfect for my Daisy," he declared.

"Yay!" The two Littles jumped up and down holding hands as they celebrated. The alert Daddies moved a few paint cans out of the way of their festivities.

When they were able to stand still again, Daisy scratched her arm. "Daddy? This paint is starting to itch."

"Me, too," Ellie agreed, rubbing her hand over the rainbow sprinkles that decorated her cheek.

"Bath time," Bear declared.

"Take the hall bathroom," he suggested to Garrett as he picked Daisy up in his arms. "Towels and washcloths are under the sink. Just make yourself at home. Yell if you need anything."

"Is the paint water-soluble?" Garrett asked, looking toward the cans.

"Oh, yeah. I had a feeling Daisy might get some on her skin and wanted an easy clean up."

"Smart."

The Littles waved at each other as their Daddies carried them to their respective bathrooms. Twenty minutes later, both Ellie and Daisy wore Bear's oversized T-shirts over freshly cleaned skin. Meeting in the kitchen, they munched on their sandwiches.

"Did you get the panic buttons installed?" Daisy asked, shivering at the memory of Daddy Leo standing in her shop. She shook her head to dismiss the mental image.

"We did. Hopefully, we put them in a handy spot for both of you. No one will know they're there except for the four of us and your employees."

Daisy lifted one hand and made a twisting motion at her mouth before throwing away the key. Her lips were sealed.

"I'll share with my employees but no one else," Ellie swore, crossing her fingers over her chest.

"We want everyone to be safe," Garrett agreed.

"Did you all go to my condo?" Daisy asked, remembering that she had asked for more clothing.

"Your Daddy was afraid of what we'd find when we got back here," Garrett shared.

"We were fine," Daisy protested.

"Decorated from head to toe but fine," Bear agreed. "I thought we'd go in a bit. That way you can pick out the clothes you want and gather your mail."

"We need to get home," Garrett announced, helping his Little hop down from her counter stool. "What do you say, Ellie?"

"Thank you for the invitation to come over and help paint. I had so much fun. Want to come over next week to help me decorate with cupcakes?" Ellie asked.

"I'd love to!"

When Bear cleared his throat, Daisy added, "I'd love to, but I need to check with my Daddy. Can I call you tomorrow?"

"Of course!" Ellie agreed before rushing forward to hug her friend. "I'll see you at work tomorrow."

"Bye!"

Daisy stood at the front door and waved as Ellie and her Daddy backed out of the driveway and disappeared from sight. "We had so much fun this afternoon."

"I'm glad, Little girl. Want to go on a clothes run?"

"Please."

"Come on. Let's get you dressed. Ellie could go home in a T-shirt. Garrett will just drive into the garage. We'll have to walk across the parking lot," he said, holding out his hand.

"You don't like me in my pretty dress?" she joked, holding the hem of Daddy's oversized T-shirt out to curtsy.

"Come on, my Little comedian. Let's put some pants on you at least," he joked, linking his fingers with hers to tow her down the hall to the nursery.

Chapter Sixteen

Twenty minutes later, they pulled into a parking spot in front of Daisy's condo. Daisy loved the stern exterior that everyone respected from her Daddy, but she also loved the way he tickled her as she scrambled out of the car, making her giggle. Not everyone knew he had a funny and sweet side, too.

"No tickles!" she protested, squirming away.

"Just trying to wake you up so you can choose clothes quickly. It's almost pumpkin time."

"Pumpkin time?"

"Remember the fairy tale when the magic disappeared at midnight and the beautiful carriage became a pumpkin?" he asked.

When she nodded, he continued, "Littles should be asleep way before that happens."

"So, I get to stay up until twelve?" Daisy asked as they approached her front door.

"No, your pumpkin time is much earlier," Bear answered. His tone did not brook any argument.

He looked past her and pointed, "Did you have something delivered?"

"No. What is that? It doesn't look like a package." Daisy rushed forward and stopped in her tracks. A battered bouquet sat on her welcome mat. As she looked up to make sure the door was locked, Daisy saw something that made her blood turn to ice inside her veins.

A red ribbon was tied around the doorknob. Daisy pointed as she struggled to string words together to tell her Daddy. Eyes glued on the tattered decoration, she backed up until her body rested against Bear's warm chest. Immediately, he wrapped his free arm around her tummy to hold her tight against him.

In a flash, he held his phone to his ear. "Detective Hazelton, Wyatt," Bear corrected himself. "Can you come to this address? Daisy's stalker has discovered where she lives." Daddy rattled off her address.

Daisy could hear the deep murmur of the policeman's voice, and she strained to hear what he said.

"The same flowers he left on her car are sitting on her doormat."

After a few more words, Bear disconnected the call. He kissed Daisy's cheek to reassure her and said, "Wyatt is on his way. He doesn't like this any more than I do."

Twisting in his arms, she watched Bear scan the area. "You have a doorbell camera. Where's the video stored?"

"I can get to it on my phone."

"Pull it up. We'll show it to Wyatt when he gets here."

Daisy fumbled with her phone. She hadn't looked at the footage since she'd first moved in and the condo management had shown her how to use the camera. It didn't help that her Daddy was watching her struggle. Finally, she remembered the password and was able to back through the recording to find it.

Her heart sank in her chest as she watched Leo Miller walk up to her door. Bear wrapped himself around her as he peered over Daisy's shoulder. The creepy guy walked up to her door and rang the doorbell. He waited for several seconds before pushing the button again. Leo didn't seem concerned that he was on video at all.

They saw him knock directly on the door—first lightly and then pound on it. He called out her name several times before shouting, "You are being very naughty, Little girl. I'm going to turn your bottom red when I get ahold of you."

Finally, he seemed to realize she wasn't at home. They watched him turn away from the camera and disappear. Daisy held her breath, hoping it was over, but he reappeared quickly with something in his hands. She watched him scatter dead blossoms over her welcome mat before pulling a ribbon out of his pocket and tying it around her door handle.

"Daisy, I don't want you to forget me. I'll find you soon. Little girls need to be taught to behave."

She breathed through her mouth, trying to fight the nausea welling inside her tummy. What was she going to do?

"I'm here. What did you find?"

The deep voice behind her made Daisy shriek with panic. Bear whirled around, immediately defensive as he pushed her behind him.

"Hey, it's just us. Sorry to startle you," the familiar figure explained, holding his hands up to defuse the panic. Avery repeated the posture just to her partner's side.

"Wyatt! Holy shit, you scared us," Bear informed him as he relaxed his stance. He nodded toward Avery. "Thanks for coming."

"Want me to leave and come back?" the detective asked with a smile.

"No. We're glad you're here. We were watching the footage from Daisy's doorbell camera. Something needs to be done about Leo Miller. He's fixated on Daisy."

"Let me see." Wyatt took Daisy's phone and rewound the video.

"How did he get your address?" Avery asked.

"That's the scary part. I don't know. He showed up at my floral shop. He just won't stop," Daisy said, trying to keep her voice even and not cry. She didn't do a very good job and stopped to sniff several times.

"Email me this video so I'll have it. We're going to pay Leo Miller a visit," Wyatt told them.

"I'd like to come with you," Bear requested.

"That can't happen. Stay away from him," Wyatt warned, holding Bear's gaze until the large man nodded.

"If he comes after her again..." Bear growled.

"We'll do everything we can to make sure that doesn't happen. We'd like to look inside, too, if you don't mind."

"Of course." Bear unlocked the front door and pushed it up.

The officers walked through her condo, making sure there was no sign of a break in. They collected the evidence and set off with warnings to be careful.

"Let's get your clothes, Little girl. Do you have a big suitcase? Let's just take anything you might need for a while," Bear urged.

While Daisy rushed to stuff the roller bag with everything she could think of, Bear cleared out anything perishable from her refrigerator and carried it to the dumpster.

"Thank you, Daddy. I don't want to come back here," Daisy confessed.

"Never by yourself," he cautioned.

Daisy nodded without argument. The last thing she wanted was to walk up to her door again. She'd never get that image out of her mind.

When her closet and drawers were emptied of all the clothes that fit and she wore frequently, Daisy struggled to fold the suitcase together.

"Let me, Little girl." Bear stepped in to muscle the sides together. "Anything else you want to take?"

Without meaning to, Daisy looked at the drawer in the

nightstand. Tearing her eyes away, she regretted not emptying that out first.

"What's in here?" Bear asked, walking to the side of the bed.

"Nothing," she answered quickly. "Just some stuff. You know—cough drops, lip balm—night stuff."

Bear opened the drawer and pulled out an electronic tablet. "You don't want to forget this. Or this," he commented, removing another item.

Daisy felt her face heat. In his large hand lay her flower-shaped vibrator. A friend had given it to her as a joke, but Daisy had fallen in love with it. It looked like the bud of a blossom, but the petals came slightly apart at the peak. The pictures on the packaging clued her in that the tip was designed to fit just around her clit. After one session experimenting with it, Daisy had grown very attached to it.

"Push your jeans and panties to your ankles, Little girl," her Daddy instructed.

"No, Daddy. It doesn't work," she lied.

With a flick of his fingers, Bear turned on the device. "Lying Little girls get consequences. Pants around your ankles. Climb up on the bed and lay on your back."

Daisy opened her mouth to argue but closed it with a snap when her Daddy shook his head. Instantly, she felt her body responding to his dominance as she became wet. Slowly, she unfastened the pants he'd dressed her in and hooked her fingers into her cotton underwear below them. Looking down at the carpet, she wiggled her hips and pushed them down to her ankles.

"Take off my pants?" she questioned.

"No, Little girl. Just climb onto the bed."

Awkwardly, Daisy waddled to the mattress and walked her hands over the comforter to the middle of the bed before hopping up on her knees. She rolled over, leaving her calves dangling over the edge of the bed.

"Stay right there." He left the room.

She could hear the cabinets banging softly in the bathroom. When he returned, he carried several towels.

Bear wrapped his hand around the material holding her legs together and lifted her feet with one hand. He tucked the towels under her bottom before lowering her onto the terrycloth material.

"Now into position," he announced as he pushed her trapped feet over her torso. He held her securely pinned to the mattress with her knees to her chest. The position displayed her completely to his view.

"Very pretty, Little girl."

"Daddy, I'll be good. Let me up," she pleaded as she watched him pick up the blossom.

"I want to see why my Little lied about her toy. There are consequences when you don't tell the truth, Daisy." He traced along her outer lips with the buzzing device.

When she squirmed as the vibrations echoed through her pelvis, he pulled it away to examine it. "Let me see. I think this pointed section could dive inside you, Daisy. Is that what it's designed to do?" he asked, looking from it to meet her gaze.

Daisy shook her head desperately.

"No lying, Little girl. I guess I'll just have to experiment a bit."

This time, her Daddy traced her inner folds. Daisy bit her lower lip, trying not to respond. When the bud's tip dipped slightly into her body, she whimpered. The vibrations spread through her body as he eased it in and out of her before pulling it away as she wilted into the mattress.

"I think there's something special here on the end. Is this supposed to fit around what I think it's designed for, Daisy?" He lowered the buzzing device between her legs once again.

Daisy jumped as his finger traced a circle around her clit. The vibration echoing through his digit made her moan. She knew what was coming.

"Daddy, no," she whimpered.

"I think you mean—Yes, Daddy," he corrected as he removed his finger and fit the carefully designed tip around the sensitive bundle of nerves.

The sensation was too much. Instantly, her body shook as an orgasm crashed over her. Daisy curled her fingers into the comforter below her as she tried to stabilize herself in a world that suddenly whirled around her.

"Daddy, stop!" she begged.

"I believe my Little girl lied to her Daddy—not once, but twice. I think your blossom vibrator needs to stay exactly where it is until I've decided you've had enough. All those wiggles moved it around a bit. Let's get it back in place."

He adjusted the device slightly. Daisy arched her neck, pressing her head into the soft padding below her. Those tingles built rapidly and in seconds, she once again climaxed hard.

"Noooo!" she wailed. His hands on her legs held her firmly in place as he watched.

"Again, Little girl," he ordered.

"No more. I can't take it."

"You'll take everything Daddy gives you. Again."

Whipping her head back in forth, she tried to deny him, but that insistent buzzing between her legs didn't stop. Again and again, she catapulted into pleasure, soaking the towels below her bottom with her juices. All thoughts and worries faded from her mind as ecstasy consumed her mind.

When he finally lifted the blossom from her body, Daisy was limp, unable to even open her eyes. "Daddy," she sighed.

"I know, Little girl. Daddy knows what you need. Sleep and I'll carry you out in a few minutes." He lowered her legs down until her thighs rested on the mattress, her jeans and panties still tangled around her ankles dangling toward the floor.

"Let me tuck you in." Bear nabbed a blanket from the rack at the side of the room and gently spread the soft material over her body.

Unable to process anything but the feeling of being cared

for completely, Daisy rolled onto her side, curling up into a ball. Safe, secure, and sated, she drifted into sleep. Aware that he moved around her, she never bothered to look. Her Daddy would take care of everything.

Chapter Seventeen

When the alarm went off the next morning, Daisy rolled away from the fiery warmth of her Daddy to look at the time. The first thing she saw was the bud-shaped vibrator on the nightstand next to her. She reached out to snag it and hide the toy in the nightstand as he obviously hit the snooze alarm, silencing the noise. A chuckle behind her made her turn quickly back to him.

"Daddy knows it's there now."

She nodded. He also knew how effective it was. Daisy hid her face against his furry chest. "I'm just going to pretend you don't."

His torso jostled underneath her as he laughed before he wrapped a warm arm around her to hold her close. "Damn, I love you," he said softly.

"I... I love you, too, Daddy," she confessed, peeking up at him. He was so good to her. He'd even carried her sleepy form to his car last night and driven her back to his house to tuck her into his bed, barely disturbing her in the process.

The scorching kiss that followed ended only when the alarm flared into action again. With a groan, she pushed away from him. "Can we just fast forward to tonight?" she suggested.

"Up, Daisy. Flowers and cupcakes are waiting for us. Is your assistant in your shop today?"

"Yes, and the delivery guy," she reassured him. "Are you going to check with Wyatt to see what happened after his talk with... that jerk?" Daisy didn't even want to say his name.

"I'll check in with him today. Go potty and I'll get you dressed."

"I can do it, Daddy," she assured him.

"I know, but Daddies like to take care of their Littles. Go." He pointed toward the bathroom, giving her a light swat to get her moving.

As she drank the strawberry smoothie he'd made for her, Daisy kept her eyes shut. Watching the video had scared her last night. And how had he held on to those dead flowers for so long? She didn't think he was going to stop just because the police talked to him.

Once inside her shop, she located the panic button that her Daddy and Garrett had installed. The hustle of the morning rush of orders distracted Daisy. Settling into her normal routine, she chatted with customers and almost stopped jumping each time the jingling bells at her door signaled a visitor. When her assistant left for lunch and TJ left to drop off a congratulatory baby arrangement, Daisy was really on edge.

The next time the bells sounded their warning, she looked up from the counter where she was transcribing an online order to see Ellie. Daisy rushed around the work surface to hug her friend who held a cupcake away safely at arm's length.

"Hi! I thought you might like to have a treat break," Ellie chirped.

"Lemon Chiffon. I'd take a break in the middle of the Valentine's Day rush for one of these." Without hesitating, she pulled off the wrapper and took a bite. "Yum!"

"You've got a little... here," Ellie laughed, pointing to her nose.

"Of course, I do. Thanks, friend. Others would have let me walk around all day long with frosting on my nose." Daisy laughed, wiping the yellow fluffy mixture off before taking another bite.

"These are so good. Is it possible they have improved even more from the first one I tried when you opened?"

"It is if someone who loves that flavor has a Daddy who's my top baker. He's been fiddling with that concoction since he met you." Ellie giggled.

"I love him," Daisy confessed, feeling tears fill her eyes as she became emotional.

"I know." Ellie rushed forward to wrap her arms around Daisy's waist. "We are so lucky we found our Daddies."

"I think your cupcakes are matchmakers. They're like a magnet pulling Daddies and Littles together," Daisy told her.

"I love that. Now, *I'm* going to cry," Ellie protested.

The two Littles clung to each other for several seconds before Ellie asked, "Who do you think will be next?"

"I don't know, but I want this for everyone." Ellie beamed at her friend. "Cupcakes and Daddies for everyone!"

"Did I hear someone ask for a Daddy?" a loathsome voice said from the doorway. His hand wrapped around the bells on the door handle to keep them quiet.

"You need to leave, Leo. No one wants you for their Daddy," Ellie said sharply after shooting a meaningful glance Daisy's way.

Daisy darted around the counter and pressed the panic button. *Please work!* She kept her eyes on Leo.

"Leo, I want you to leave and never come back. I have a Daddy now. Even if I didn't, you wouldn't be on my list of a million possibilities to replace him."

"That's rude, Little girl." Leo stalked forward to circle the counter.

"Stop!" Daisy reached under the counter to press the button again. Her fingers knocked a heavy glass vase over and she grabbed it. Raising it with both hands, she crashed it down on Leo's head as he got close.

For a minute, she didn't think it had worked. Then, his eyes rolled up in his head and he dropped like a rock to the ground. "Help me tie him up with this ribbon," she shouted to Ellie as she pulled a long length from the spool on the counter.

It wasn't thick but would hold if they wrapped it around his hands multiple times. Daringly moving close to the dangerous man, they secured his hands first before starting to work on his feet.

The door slammed open, making both women jump away. Bear filled the doorway. Waves of violence emanated from him. Military training was evident in every line of his body. He was there to destroy anyone who threatened his Little.

"Daisy!"

"I'm okay, Daddy." She knelt carefully at Leo's feet, avoiding the shattered glass on the floor to finish tying the ribbon, only to feel herself lifted into the air.

"Are you hurt?" he demanded.

When she shook her head no, he ordered, "Wait over there," before taking over the job of wrapping ribbon around Leo's ankles.

The sound of distant sirens penetrated the glass picture window as tires squealed to a stop at the curb. Again, the door slammed open as Garrett burst into the room.

"You okay, Rainbow?" he asked frantically, running his hands over Ellie.

"Yes, Daddy. Daisy knocked Leo out and we tied him up."

"You did what?" Bear growled, looking at Daisy as he stood up.

"When I hit the panic button, I touched a vase. I didn't think. I just smashed it over his head." Daisy pointed to the glass crunching under his feet on the floor.

"Oh, no, Daddy! You got cut." She pointed to a trickle of blood running down from Bear's knee.

"Ellie, run into the back and get the first aid kit on the wall." Daisy pushed her Daddy toward the picture window so she could see his leg better.

By the time the squad car pulled to a stop at the curb, Daisy had wiped the glass shard from his skin and disinfected it. When her Daddy moved toward the door, she wrapped her arms around his leg.

"No, Daddy. Let me put a bandage on first," she demanded.

As the police entered cautiously, Daisy considered the scene through their eyes: a man unconscious on the floor with a mile of red ribbon securing his hands and feet, a woman in a Blooms by Daisy polo shirt applying a large cartoon frog bandage on a massive man's leg, another couple huddled close by, and a half-eaten, bright yellow cupcake and broken glass trampled all over the floor.

"Hi, folks. It looks like we missed all the fun," the patrolman suggested. "Want to tell me what happened?"

Twenty minutes later, a groggy Leo sat in the back of the patrol car, muttering about Littles who are too much trouble and his plans to move. Wyatt had appeared after the first responders. He entered the shop as Garrett swept up the glass.

"I think that's the last you'll see of Leo," Wyatt announced.

"Really?" Daisy asked, studying his face.

"I didn't want to suggest it, but most harassers back way off when the victim fights back. Leo's looking for a Little to control. You two just showed him how kickass Littles can be," Wyatt said with dancing eyes.

He laughed as Ellie and Daisy high fived each other. Sobering, he added, "That doesn't mean I don't want you in my self-defense class. This could have gone very, very wrong. You were extremely lucky."

Daisy and Ellie nodded and returned to their Daddies' arms.

Erica suddenly appeared in the doorway. "What happened? All the workers in every store are standing out on the curb."

"I think I'm going to need you to order more ribbon," Daisy said with a laugh before telling her assistant what had happened.

The police cars pulled away from the shop, carrying Leo down to the station.

"Crap! The cupcakes!" Bear shouted before dashing to the door. He turned back to meet Daisy's eyes. "Are you okay here by yourself?"

"Erica's here. And I'm good. Go save the cupcakes," Daisy said, shooing him out the door. She realized she did feel good.

Garrett steered Ellie outside at a more sedate rate as customers trickled into the florist shop. Employees from different shops dropped in to send flowers to friends and relatives. Daisy knew they really were there to find out what had happened and support her business. She thanked everyone for being concerned about her.

By the end of the day when she turned the sign to CLOSED, Daisy was exhausted. She walked out of the shop on the way to her car, but it wasn't alone. Her Daddy was parked right next to it.

As she approached, he got out to come wrap his arms around her. "Ready to go home?"

"I could go back to my condo."

"Not a chance. You're coming home with me. Take pity on a poor Daddy. Don't make me worry about you."

"If you need me, I'd like to be with you, too."

"I'm always going to need you. Let's go home and make some plans." When she nodded, he added, "And snuggle. Daddy's heart needs snuggles."

"Me, too," she chimed in, smiling at him.

"Do you remember the way?" he teased.

"I'll follow you," she replied, knowing it would challenge her brain to concentrate.

"Sounds good." Bear helped her into her car before warning, "Drive carefully."

"Yes, Daddy."

Chapter Eighteen

"Eat your green beans," her Daddy instructed, pointing at the last thing on her plate.

"I don't really like veggies," she protested.

"Veggies keep you in vase-smashing shape. Besides, you liked the veggie salad I made you the other day, remember? Let's make them more fun."

Bear stood and pulled a bottle of ranch dressing from the refrigerator. He poured a dollop of the thick white mixture onto her plate.

"Wait! You need one more thing." He opened a drawer to pull out a pair of chopsticks attached at the top.

"I don't know how to use those," she protested.

"Don't tell anyone, but neither do I. These are cheater chopsticks."

He showed her how to use them and said, "Try it out. Pick up a green bean and dip it into the dressing. See if you like it better."

Carefully, Daisy trapped one of the slim veggies and tapped the tip into the white mixture. Lifting it to her lips, she took the smallest bite possible.

"Yum! That's good. Maybe I like green beans," she enthused, dipping it back into the ranch dressing.

"Maybe you should listen to your Daddy more often," he pointed out, one brow lifted even though he was also grinning.

"I like the chopsticks, too, Daddy. I think I'll use them more often."

He chuckled. "You'd be skin and bones by the end of the week if you tried that, considering how slow you're able to eat with them."

She giggled and stuffed another green bean into her mouth.

He sat back and watched as she finished her dinner.

She loved his cooking and the fact that he nearly always made dinner for her, but she really liked the evenings when they got home too late and he didn't have enough time to feed her, because on those nights, he let her be even younger.

When they were home, Daisy was always Little, but her age range wavered greatly. Some nights she was older. Some nights she was younger.

This extended to everything. Sometimes he told her to go take a shower. Sometimes he washed her himself in the tub. He even had bubbles and bath toys.

Bath, bottle, and diaper evenings were her favorite, but she hadn't had the gumption to tell him that. He'd said he enjoyed when she was younger, and she believed him, but she knew he didn't fully realize she preferred it and wished he would let her be younger more often.

It was embarrassing to admit. She wasn't sure many of her friends spent as much time as her in a younger mindset. She knew Ellie wore diapers sometimes just like Daisy, but how often?

Daisy loved her Daddy so much, and she didn't want to rock the boat by complaining. She was the luckiest Little girl in the world. Why should she want more? He already gave her so much.

She was well aware that assuming a younger role was a lot

more work for Bear. He had to take the time to rock her and feed her and bathe her and change her diaper. He worked long hours just like she did. It would be rude to ask him to spend his precious time off caring for her at a deeper level.

Daddy's voice interrupted her pity party, jerking her back to the present. "What's going on in your pretty head, Daisy?"

She pushed around the last few green beans with the chopsticks and shrugged. "Nothing."

He leaned forward and put his elbows on the table. "I'm not buying that, Baby girl. Not for a second. You've been deep in thought for ten minutes, no longer eating. And you look sad."

She swallowed hard and dropped her chopsticks.

"Daisy..." he warned. "Talk to Daddy."

She shook her head. "It's nothing, Daddy. I swear." She didn't want to tell him what she was thinking. It wasn't fair to him. She wouldn't burden him with her problems.

Bear stood from the table and reached for their plates to carry them to the dishwasher. He silently loaded everything and put away the leftovers.

Daisy sat very still in her seat and watched him. She'd never seen him this quiet. He wasn't giving her any indication what he was thinking. Was he mad? She couldn't be sure. He probably should be but she'd never seen him angry. Not with her at least.

She was being naughty, though.

When he was finished, he turned around, leaned against the counter, and crossed his arms over his chest. He stared at her for a long time. "It bothers me that you won't tell me what's on your mind, Daisy."

"I'm sorry, Daddy." She glanced down at her lap and fidgeted. Why hadn't she realized she was so deep in her head that he'd noticed she was thinking so hard? "It's not a big deal. I promise."

"I think you should let me be the judge of that, Baby girl."

She tried to think of something she could say to appease him. "I was just thinking about the green beans and wondering if maybe I could dip other vegetables into ranch dressing. I bet they would taste good that way, too." She glanced up at him hopefully.

His brows rose high on his head and he blinked at her. "Now you're insulting me, Daisy." His voice was hurt. "I think you should go sit in your naughty chair in your nursery until you're willing to tell Daddy the truth."

Daisy sucked in a breath. She'd hoped to never need that naughty chair, but there was no doubt she'd earned it tonight. She'd kept secrets from Daddy and lied to him.

She slid off the chair and shuffled toward her nursery, heading straight for the corner and dropping onto the chair, facing the wall. Tears welled up in the corners of her eyes and she swiped them away.

The phrases Daddy had painted on the walls jumped out at her. *Think Twice, I Love You, Be Good*. She definitely should have thought twice about lying to Daddy. She hoped he still loved her after she'd treated him with such disrespect. She was certainly not being a good girl.

The only thing worse than not telling Daddy what she'd been thinking was disappointing him. It weighed heavily on her.

Daddy didn't come into the room for a long time. She wondered if he was watching her from the hallway. She wasn't sure. Sadness crept in deeper with every passing minute. She'd alienated him and insulted him and hurt his feelings. That wasn't a very nice girl.

She sniffled as tears fell again. She didn't have any tissues, so she lifted the corner of her T-shirt to wipe her eyes. She felt confined and restricted in the tight jeans, panties, bra, and T-shirt she'd worn to work.

Obviously, there was no way to avoid putting on adult clothes for the hours she was at work every day. She had no choice but to be an adult while running a business. But she just wanted to shed those things when she got home and not have to think about anything.

Couldn't he see that she preferred being super Little? Why couldn't he read her mind? She furrowed her brow and kicked at the wall with her socked feet, frustrated.

She was behaving like a toddler, and she knew it, but she couldn't stop it. It was beyond irrational for her to be mad at Daddy for not reading her mind.

Maybe he *did* know she wanted to be younger and he simply didn't enjoy it as much as she did. She needed to be willing to compromise. She certainly couldn't end a relationship simply because she was greedy and wanted him to do *everything* for her. That wasn't fair.

She shuddered at the thought of ending this relationship. It was the furthest thing from her mind. She loved Bear with all her heart. They'd been talking about ending her lease because she never went to her condo anymore.

He wouldn't suggest she move in with him permanently if he didn't love her back. She knew he did. He'd told her he loved her. He wouldn't say it if he didn't mean it.

Daisy sniffled again and then the tears really started falling. She couldn't stop them as they turned into sobs that weren't quiet. She was a mess of emotions and sadness when strong hands suddenly landed on her shoulders.

She tipped her head to one side when Daddy handed her several tissues. "Get it all out, Baby girl," he encouraged. "I'm going to go sit in the rocking chair. When you're ready to talk, I'd like you to come sit on my lap."

He released her shoulders, and she immediately missed his touch. She liked it when he was touching her. Even her shoulders. Or just her hand. That was part of why she liked to role play at a younger age—because he touched her more. He held her while he fed her and had no choice but to put his hands all over her when he changed her and bathed her.

She not only liked his touch, but she had to admit she got more aroused in her younger mindset than any other time, too. Was something wrong with her?

She kept crying as if her world was coming to an end. In a way, she felt like it was. She needed to come clean with her Daddy, but what if he didn't want the same things as her and they couldn't agree and this was it? The end of their relationship.

She shivered as she wiped her tears again and blew her nose. It was time to stop being a big baby and face her Daddy. Ironic. *Stop being a baby.* That was exactly what she didn't *want* to stop.

Sucking up the last of her sniffles, she found the strength to stand. She needed to be brave and tell her Daddy what was on her mind. No matter what.

He reached for her the moment she met his gaze. "Come here, Baby girl." His voice was gentle and loving. She didn't deserve his kindness, and she almost started crying all over again.

Instead, she ran across the room and let him lift her onto his lap. She hugged him tightly around the neck for a long time, loving the way he rubbed her back and smoothed his hand down her hair.

He kissed her temple several times, too. Finally, he spoke. "It makes Daddy very sad that you're so unhappy, Baby girl. It breaks my heart. I want to help you, but you have to tell me how."

She released her tight grip and settled in his lap. "I'm sorry, Daddy. I didn't mean to be naughty. I didn't want to bother you with my problems. You already do so much for me. You're the bestest Daddy in the world. I don't want to be a greedy girl who can't be happy with what she has."

He stopped rocking and stiffened. "Is there something you don't have that you need, Baby girl? Because if it's within my means, I'll buy it for you in a heartbeat. Surely you know that."

She shook her head. "It's not a *thing*, Daddy. It doesn't cost money."

He tipped her head back and met her gaze. His eyes were furrowed in confusion. "Please tell Daddy what's going on. My heart is breaking."

She swallowed hard and licked her lips. "I love everything about our relationship. I swear I do, Daddy. You're the—"

He shook his head. "Bestest Daddy in the world? You already said that."

She nodded. "Yeah. I guess I did."

"And yet. I must not be quite the very bestest, bestest Daddy because I've missed a cue and I'm not fulfilling a need, am I?"

She looked down, hating herself.

He waited.

Finally, she took a deep breath and spit it out. "I want to be younger more of the time, Daddy."

He flinched. "You want to be younger?" He rubbed her lower back. "You mean like when you take a bottle and wear a diaper?"

She nodded, glad she hadn't been forced to say those words. He'd done it for her.

He tucked his finger under her chin and lifted her face. "Why on earth couldn't you just tell me that, Daisy? I know you enjoy playing at a younger age, but I didn't realize it was that important to you or that you preferred it more often."

"Because it's so much work for you, Daddy. You work hard all day and sometimes at Blaze in the evenings, too. I don't want you to have to take care of me so totally when you're only off work a few hours in the evening."

He frowned. "What if that's what I prefer? Did you ever think maybe I like it when you're younger as much as you do?" He glanced around the room. "Why do you think I have a nursery with a crib and bottles and diapers if I don't want you to use them?"

"I know you enjoy it, but it's not something we do every night, so I assumed you were too tired some nights to deal with me."

"Deal with you?" His voice rose. He was angry, or perhaps hurt. "Daisy, dealing with you is the greatest pleasure in my life. I've waited forever to find the perfect Baby girl who checks off every box on my list. That's you, Daisy. In every way."

She wanted to believe him.

He gave her a slight shake of the hips. "Daisy, you're my life. You've brought sunshine and laughter and...yellow into my days." He gave her a small smile. "You make my heart beat faster and fill my soul every time I look at you."

She took a deep breath.

"I didn't want to pressure you to spend more time younger. I was trying to take my cues from you. You never ask me for diapers and bottles, so I assumed I was pressuring you on those things."

"I'm sorry, Daddy."

He smiled a little bigger. "I think we had a breakdown in communication." He patted her bottom. "Here I was, hoping one day you would decide you liked to be younger at home, and you were wishing for the same thing. We're quite the pair."

Her eyes widened.

He nodded. "Yeah, I'm just as much to blame. I should have told you I preferred when you were younger. I didn't want you to do something you weren't comfortable with just for me, though."

"I didn't want to ask you to invest even more time in me. I know it's a lot, caring for me when I'm younger."

He squeezed her. "I love caring for you. I'd rather be caring for you than anything in the world. It's invigorating. Even if I'm tired after a long day, the idea of caring for you perks me up and gives me a second wind."

She smiled cautiously. "Yeah?"

"Yeah." He quickly stood her on her feet, so fast she almost toppled over backward, but he held her steady with his hands on her hips. "Let's get these clothes off you."

She grinned. "I hate them."

He chuckled. "Even at work?"

"Yes, but I tolerate them at work. I don't have a choice. I flip a switch in my head and go into adult-mode. But when I get home..."

"You just want Daddy to get you out of these tight jeans and panties and bra and let you be my Baby girl." His voice was soft as he popped the button on her jeans and lowered the zipper.

"Yes, Daddy."

He lowered the jeans and her panties down her legs and then bent to help her step out of them and pull off her socks.

After ridding her of the bottom half of her clothes, he pulled her shirt over her head and unfastened her bra.

She breathed out the moment he had her naked as if she'd been unable to take a full breath until now.

Daddy cupped her breasts and thumbed her nipples reverently. "Sex, bath, bottle, diaper, bed? How's that sound?"

She grinned and nodded eagerly. "I love that plan, Daddy."

He slid his hands down to her hips. "From now on, when we get home from work, first thing I'll do is remove your clothes and put a diaper on you. We can get some more play clothes that are appropriate for your age, too. Maybe some more loose dresses. You can wear leggings over your diaper when it's cold. How does that sound?"

"Perfect." She reached for the front of his shirt and played with the soft cotton. "It's not too much work?"

"Never." He kissed her forehead. "You're never too much work. I'd love nothing more than to take care of your every need when we're home." He kissed her lips next.

She smiled. "Maybe sometimes when we go out like to other Little's houses or the club, I'll be slightly older, but when we're home..."

"Understood." He lifted her chin again. His expression was serious again. "From now on, when something is bothering you, I want you to tell Daddy. Don't let it bottle up inside you so you end up crying in the naughty corner."

"Yes, Daddy." She never wanted to go on that emotional roller coaster again. It was awful.

Chapter Nineteen

Bear spun Daisy around by her shoulders and patted her bottom. "Head for Daddy's bedroom."

She didn't have to be told twice. She nearly skipped the short distance until she reached his bed. She was about to climb onto it when his hands landed on her hips and she was lifted off the floor.

She squealed. "*Daddy.*"

"I didn't want you to fall, Baby girl. It's safer if Daddy lifts you up onto the bed. It's pretty high."

She giggled as she spun around and scooted toward the center, watching him undress. He was exaggerating of course, but he was giving her what she wanted. To be treated like she was too young to climb up on her own.

She gasped when he revealed his cock as if she'd never seen it before. Was it larger than usual today?

They'd had sex many times, but she was shivering as if this would be their first time together. He was so big and strong. She loved that about him. How tall and broad he was. It wasn't a requirement for being a Daddy of course, but it didn't hurt that he looked like the giant bear he was.

When he was fully naked, he simply stood in front of her,

watching her, his cock bobbing in front of him. He fisted his hands at his sides and took deep breaths.

"You take my breath away, Daisy. You're the prettiest Baby girl I've ever seen. I could stand here and stare at you all night."

She flushed and opened her legs. "I'd rather you climb up here and touch me, Daddy. It's your touch I crave more than anything. I think that's why I prefer to be younger. You have to touch me more to take care of me when I'm too young to do so myself."

He gave her a slow sexy smile. "Oh, Baby girl... You shouldn't have told Daddy that last part. I'll never put you down between work and morning from now on. I'll hold you in my arms, carry you on my hip, and snuggle against you in bed. You'll be so tired of me you'll take those words back in less than a week."

She giggled and shook her head. "Never. Please stop teasing me and start the touching part."

He chuckled as he rolled on a condom before he climbed onto the bed, grabbed her thighs, and lowered his face between her legs. He suckled her so deep and fast that she gasped. He thrust his tongue into her and then flicked it over her clit until she was dizzy.

"Daddy..." she moaned.

He lifted his face to meet her gaze. "Had enough of my touch yet, Baby girl?" he teased.

She shook her head.

He licked a path up her tummy, making her shiver, and then sucked one of her nipples, tormenting it with his tongue and teeth before switching to the other to repeat the same thing.

She was gasping when he finally found her lips and kissed her deeper than he'd ever done before.

She melted under him, grabbing his hips and digging her blunt nails into his skin. "*Daddy*," she cried out when he broke the kiss and lined his cock up with her entrance. "Please..."

He thrust into her, making her gasp, but then he met her

gaze and cupped her face. "Eyes on mine, Baby girl." He eased in and out of her languidly, letting the need build until she thought she'd lose her mind from the teasing.

He didn't stop though. He simply changed the angle so that the base of his erection hit her clit just right, making her moan. When her eyes rolled back, he didn't comment except to kiss her neck. "Come, Baby girl."

She did as he demanded, her orgasm rushing through her body so fast it took her by surprise. While her pussy was milking his cock, he followed her over the edge on a low groan that sounded like a slice of heaven. Her heaven.

He hovered over her, panting, for a long time before lifting his face and meeting her gaze again. "I love you, Daisy. I love everything about you. I love your adult self who is so strong and confident and hardworking. I love your Little self who likes to color and play with her friends at Blaze. But most of all, I love your Baby self who's willing to turn over her care to me."

He stroked her cheeks with his thumbs and continued, "It's humbling to receive the gift you're giving me. The gift of submission. A gift I will not take for granted. I promise to do everything in my power to make sure your needs are always met."

She licked her dry lips. "I promise to always tell you what those needs are. And you have to tell me if you need a change, too, Daddy," she challenged.

"Of course, Baby girl. That's the only way this will work. Open communication. Just because you crave a deeper level of submission when we're home right now doesn't mean you'll always want to be that young so often. That's okay."

"It won't make you sad if I change my mind?"

"Nope. It will make me sad if you don't tell me how you're feeling. I'm in love with all of Daisy. Everything about her. That will never change. No matter what our age play looks like from day to day, I'll always be in love with you."

"I'll always be in love with you too, Daddy."

He kissed her lips again. "Are you ready for a bath now?"

"Will you get in with me, Daddy?"

"I love that idea. Will you share your boats?"

She giggled. "You can have the blue one. I want the yellow one."

He chuckled, the vibrations extending up her body. "I'll always save the yellow one for you, Baby girl."

"You don't have to save every yellow thing for me, Daddy. I don't like yellow squash for example." She curled up her nose.

He laughed. "I bet it tastes good if you dip it in ranch."

She shrugged. "Maybe. Probably only if I use chopsticks, though. They made the green beans taste better."

He stared at her, smiling like a loon. She knew she reflected back the same expression. She was so happy. Happier than she'd ever imagined was possible.

Tarson, Bear, Teddy had a lot of names, but to her, he was just Daddy. Her Daddy. She planned to hold on to him forever.

Author's Note

We hope you're enjoying Little Cakes! We are so excited to be working together to create this new series! More stories will be coming soon!

Little Cakes:
(by Pepper North and Paige Michaels)
Rainbow Sprinkles
Lemon Chiffon
Blue Raspberry
Red Velvet
Pink Lemonade
Black Forest
Witch's Brew
Pumpkin Spice
Santa's Kiss
Fudge Crunch
Sweet Tooth
Flirty Kumquat
Birthday Cake
Caramel Drizzle

AUTHOR'S NOTE

Maraschino Cherry
Reindeer Tracks

About Pepper North

Ever just gone for it? That's what *USA Today* Bestselling Author Pepper North did in 2017 when she posted a book for sale on Amazon without telling anyone. Thanks to her amazing fans, the support of the writing community, Mr. North, and a killer schedule, she has now written more than 70 books!

Enjoy contemporary, paranormal, dark, and erotic romances that are both sweet and steamy? Pepper will convert you into one of her loyal readers. What's coming in the future? A Daddypalooza!

Connect with me on your favorite platform!
I'm also having fun on TikTok as well!

- amazon.com/author/pepper_north
- bookbub.com/profile/pepper-north
- facebook.com/AuthorPepperNorth
- instagram.com/4peppernorth
- pinterest.com/4peppernorth
- twitter.com/@4peppernorth

Pepper North Series

Dr. Richards' Littles®

A beloved age play series that features Littles who find their forever Daddies and Mommies. Dr. Richards guides and supports their efforts to keep their Littles happy and healthy.

Available on Amazon

SANCTUM

Pepper North introduces you to an age play community that is isolated from the surrounding world. Here Littles can be Little, and Daddies can care for their Littles and keep them protected from the outside world.

Available on Amazon

Soldier Daddies

What private mission are these elite soldiers undertaking? They're all searching for their perfect Little girl.

Available on Amazon

The Keepers

This series from Pepper North is a twist on contemporary age play romances. Here are the stories of humans cared for by specially selected Keepers of an alien race. These are science fiction novels that age play readers will love!

Available on Amazon

The Magic of Twelve

The Magic of Twelve features the stories of twelve women transported on their 22nd birthday to a new life as the droblin (cherished Little one) of a Sorcerer of Bairn. These magic wielders have waited a long time to take complete care of their droblin's needs. They will protect their precious one to their last drop of magic from a growing menace. Each novel is a complete story.

Available on Amazon

About Paige Michaels

Paige Michaels is a USA Today bestselling author of naughty romance books that are meant to make you squirm. She loves a happily ever after and spends the bulk of every day either reading erotic romance or writing it.

Other books by Paige Michaels:

The Nurturing Center:
Susie
Emmy
Jenny
Lily
Annie
Mindy

Eleadian Mates:
His Little Emerald
His Little Diamond
His Little Garnet
His Little Amethyst
His Little Sapphire
His Little Topaz

Littleworld:
Anabel's Daddy
Melody's Daddy

Haley's Daddy
Willow's Daddy
Juliana's Daddy
Tiffany's Daddy
Felicity's Daddy
Emma's Daddy
Lizzy's Daddy
Claire's Daddy
Kylie's Daddy
Ruby's Daddy
Briana's Daddies
Jake's Mommy and Daddy
Luna's Daddy
Petra's Daddy
Littleworld Box Set One
Littleworld Box Set Two
Littleworld Box Set Three
Littleworld Box Set Four

Holidays at Rawhide Ranch:
Felicity's Little Father's Day
A Cheerful Little Coloring Day

If you'd like to see a map of Regression island where Littleworld is located, please visit my website: PaigeMichaels.com

facebook.com/PaigeMichaelsAuthor
amazon.com/author/PaigeMichaels
bookbub.com/authors/paige-michaels

Afterword

If you've enjoyed this story, it will make our day if you could leave an honest review on Amazon. Reviews help other people find our books and help us continue creating more Little adventures. Our thanks in advance. We always love to hear from our readers what they enjoy and dislike when reading an alternate love story featuring age-play.

Made in the USA
Monee, IL
14 December 2024